Callie slumped to her haunches. "How are we going to do this?"

"Do what?" Shep woofed.

"Survive," she snuffled. "We haven't even been Outside a full sun, and we only have one bowl of water and a single bag of kibble."

Shep licked her nose and wagged his tail. "We'll think of something," he said, grinning. "Or, better yet, you'll think of something and I'll nose everyone into doing it."

Callie smiled. "Go team," she woofed.

DOGS OF THE **DROWNED CITY**

DOGS OF THE DROWNED CITY

THE PACK

DOGS OF THE DROWNED CITY

BY DAYNA LORENTZ

SCHOLASTIC INC.

NEW YORK   TORONTO   LONDON   AUCKLAND

SYDNEY   MEXICO CITY   NEW DELHI   HONG KONG

Text copyright © 2012 by Dayna Lorentz

All rights reserved. Published by Scholastic Inc.
SCHOLASTIC and associated logos are trademarks and/or registered trademarks of Scholastic Inc.

No part of this publication may be reproduced, stored in a retrieval system, or transmitted in any form or by any means, electronic, mechanical, photocopying, recording, or otherwise, without written permission of the publisher. For information regarding permission, write to Scholastic Inc., Attention: Permissions Department, 557 Broadway, New York, NY 10012.

ISBN 978-0-545-27646-7

12 11 10 9 8 7 6 5 4 3 2 1   12 13 14 15 16 17/0

Printed in the U.S.A.   40
First printing, May 2012

FOR MOM, DAD, AND JORDAN

CHAPTER 1
THE NEW WORLD

The blinding lights of the fight cage shone down on Shep once again. But no men rattled the links of the cage: The fight ring was surrounded only by dogs — wild dogs. The stench of them overwhelmed every other scent.

The wild dogs parted, and Zeus strode through their ranks, then sprang into the cage.

"I have new friends," he snarled.

Before Zeus could strike, a river crashed into the fight ring. Shep struggled against the pull of the raging waters. His paws dug at the roiling river, white froth splashing with each slash of his claws.

"You can't save us all," Zeus growled.

Shep saw his friend sink below him. Shep dove down, but could not catch Zeus's paw with his teeth.

I've failed him, Shep thought. *I've failed them all.*

A high-pitched shriek deafened him. A horde of wild dogs rose up from the river bottom, became the river. Shep's paws slapped against their fur. Their teeth scraped along his hide.

"We rise again!" Zeus howled, emerging from the river of dogs like a bird, floating higher and higher, expanding until he covered the sky like a storm.

"Shep." A squeaky voice interrupted his nightmare. "Stop kicking!"

Shep cracked open his eyelids. The little dachshund pup, Oscar, was struggling to untangle himself from Shep's legs.

"Hold on, pup," Shep woofed, lifting his forepaws.

Oscar tumbled onto the overturned wooden box they'd been sleeping on, landing flat on his belly. "Sheesh," he yipped. "You have some crazy dreams."

Shep rolled onto his paws and slowly pushed himself up. "I know," he groaned. "Believe me, pup, I know."

Now that he was standing, Shep's body reminded him of all he'd been through in the last few suns, since being abandoned by his family. Escaping his den, rescuing other trapped dogs, fighting for his life, half drowning in the torrent of the wave — each one was a distinct pain. His jaw ached from turning knobs, his paw throbbed from Kaz's bite, and pain radiated from his shoulder where Zeus had thrown him to the floor. His skin felt stiff and his fur was crusty with salt. *I wish it had all just been a dream*, Shep thought.

Oscar stretched beside him. Shep had promised to protect the pup from the Black Dog — from the chaos of the wild, from death itself. Looking Outside, Shep hoped he could make good on that promise. The wall of the kibble den had been torn away, giving him a clear view of the street beyond. A tree lay on its side, its roots a disk of broken bristles. Cars rested with their roofs against the stone or hunched, backs broken, beneath chunks of debris. Drifts of sand leaned against every obstacle in the wave's path, though the wave itself had been reduced to puddles, which glimmered on every surface.

Callie stood near the overturned Car that marked where the window hole had once been. The other dogs stood near her, huddled in clumps. Dover the old black Lab licked his tail — it must've still hurt from where Shep had accidentally dropped the plank on it the sun before. *Thanks for reminding me*, Shep grumbled silently.

The greyhound, Snoop, and the English setter, Wensleydale, called Cheese for short, played with a half-deflated Ball they'd dug out of the rubble. Their long, narrow bodies swatted about as they tugged on the plastic. Daisy the pug leapt at the flattened Ball, barking about how it was her turn to play with it.

Boji the yellow Lab licked a wound that Virgil (terrier, Airedale class) had suffered during the battle with the wild dogs. Nearby, Ginny the sheltie was yapping at Rufus the schnauzer about her hero, some dog named Lassie who'd visited her every sun through the light-window.

Higgins, of the Brussels griffon line, sat on a brightly colored plastic box watching the others, his bushy furface all aquiver. *Probably taking notes for his dog-breed research.*

The wood box creaked as Shep hopped off it, and all the dogs' eyes were instantly on him. Cheese froze with his jaws clamped down on the Ball, and Daisy hung off the other end of it by her snaggleteeth, her front paws dangling. Dover stopped licking his tail. Ginny paused mid-yap concerning the way the sun would flicker across Lassie's coat. They looked at Shep expectantly, waiting for him to tell them what to do. Or, to be more precise, for Callie to tell Shep what he should tell them all to do.

Shep gave them each a nod of the snout as he passed, and padded to Callie's side. "That was the den shrieking, right?" he asked. "I heard it in my dream as the howls of wild dogs."

Callie licked his nose. "Don't worry. The building's not attacking us," she yipped. "At least, not yet."

It was just after dawn, and pinkish light colored the few clouds that remained in the sky. The storm itself was nowhere to be scented; the sky was clear as glass and the air dry and still. At street level, the salty smell of the wave covered everything; in some directions, the salt scent was stronger, signaling that the wave water had not completely retreated. Chemical smells leached from the toppled Cars and broken buildings. The stench of death and decay had grown overnight. Swarms of flies buzzed over gruesome mounds of — Shep didn't want to find out. All the dogs were careful

4

to stay inside the hollowed remains of the kibble den, afraid to set paw in this new world.

Shep decided the best way to get everyone out of the den before it collapsed around them was to suggest food. "Any dog have an idea of where to get some kibble?" he woofed.

The squaredog, Rufus, stood and shook his short, silver coat. "If we knew where to get kibble," he yapped, "you think we'd be sitting here nibbling our paws?"

In some ways, the world had not changed. Rufus's natural state was that of a tail dragger. Even when things were going well — they'd just survived a world-crushing wave, for Great Wolf's sake! — he was a downer dog.

"Any dog else?" Shep groaned.

Snoop bounded up to Shep, knocking over Oscar and slapping Callie in the snout with his tail. "Shep-there's-mice-and-rats-and-rabbits-all-up-on-the-second-floor-maybe-they-have-kibble-Shep-whaddya-think-huh?"

Cheese dropped the Ball, and Daisy with it. "I think I did smell something like kibble up on the balcony."

"Well, then, what are we waiting for?" yapped Ginny. "In Lassie's name, let's eat!"

The little sheltie flounced off the white box she'd been perched on and bounded up the stairs, with Rufus, Cheese, Daisy, Snoop, and Virgil on her tail.

Callie's tail dropped. "This is a bad idea."

Higgins tilted his head. "You wouldn't think a pug could hop up stairs like that," he snuffled.

Little Oscar stood with his fat forepaws on the bottom step, trying to pull himself up onto it.

"Boji, can you carry me?" he whimpered.

Boji trotted to the pup's side, but shied away from the step like it had growled at her. "Oh, dear," she whined. "Perhaps the others will bring us down some kibble?"

Again, the shrieking metal sound echoed around the den.

"That's not good," woofed Callie. She sniffed the air, then the remnants of the window wall. "Not good at all."

Dover angled his snout toward Shep's ear. "Should you maybe bark for them to come back down?"

There was another shriek, and this time the floor trembled.

"What's happening, Callie?" barked Shep. He felt a vibration in his paws.

The bottommost step cracked in half with a bang.

"The steps!" howled Boji. "I knew they were after us!" She grabbed Oscar by the scruff and bolted for the Outside.

The whole room shuddered. Then, with a loud groan, the second floor dropped a stretch. The dogs who'd already climbed up screamed with fear.

Shep raced to the bottom of the stairs. "Come back!" he barked.

The dogs scrambled toward his bark, leaping down the steps, first Ginny, then Snoop. The stairs jolted, cracks appearing on all sides now, just as Virgil and Daisy raced past Shep's flank. Then the steps split in two: The part connected to the second level bent backward, then dropped onto the main floor and burst into pieces. Four steps rose in front of Shep, leading to nothing. An empty space, a bit more than a stretch across, separated the top remaining step from the sloping second story. At its edge stood Cheese and Rufus.

Callie raced to Shep's side. "We have to save them," she yipped quietly. She glared at the second floor, as if willing it to toss over the other dogs unharmed. "Cheese," she called, "can you jump the space carrying Rufus in your jaws?"

Cheese nosed the gray squaredog in the side. "He's too heavy," Cheese woofed.

The floor trembled and groaned, then dropped another stretch. Rufus yelped, scrambling backward. Cheese hooked a paw onto a shelf and pulled himself to firmer ground. He bit Rufus's scruff and dragged him away from the edge.

"You should get your tails out of here!" Cheese barked. "We'll find another way!"

"Don't leave me!" yelped Rufus.

"We're a pack," Callie snapped. "We don't leave dogs behind."

Shep sniffed the edge of the step. "We could smell if there are any beds left, anything soft. We could pile them where the steps used to be, like we did to get off the grate back at our dens."

Callie squinted her brown eyes. "No," she woofed, "we don't have time."

The balcony screeched like a startled tomcat.

"Cheese!" Callie barked. "You have to grab Rufus by the scruff and throw him over!"

Rufus squealed as if he'd been smacked. "Have you lost your tail?" he yelped.

Callie sprang like a squirrel from a branch, leaping from the stairs onto the second floor. Her claws scraped the slanting surface for several agonizing heartbeats before, finally, catching hold. Shep and the others were shocked to silence.

Callie snapped her teeth at Rufus. "Stop being a tail dragger! I just leapt the gap. Now you do it!" Callie's tail stood high and her jowls curled to reveal her sharp, white teeth.

The squaredog must have been too bewildered to protest, because he raced back, then jumped over the rift, paws flailing. Shep reached out and snapped his teeth around Rufus's scruff, dragging him onto the steps.

Shep dropped the squaredog on the solid stone and heaved several breaths. "Callie, you crazy yapper!" he howled.

Callie scrambled back a stretch, then flew over the gap, soaring like a hawk, and landed beside Shep. "He's off the balcony, isn't he?" she woofed, as if nothing completely fur-brained had just happened.

Cheese jumped the span easily. Just as his paws touched the step, the whole second floor shuddered. The stone gave one final jerk, then collapsed. The front edge of the balcony crashed down onto the main floor, creating a giant ramp.

"We should have waited," Rufus yapped. "I wouldn't have had to jump!"

Callie nipped Rufus on the neck. "Let's get out of here before the roof falls on our snouts!"

The four dogs charged Outside. When they reached the

Sidewalk, Callie turned to look back at the kibble den. Her snout split into a wide smile, and her tongue lolled between her jaws. "We're lucky we made it through the night," she woofed cheerfully between pants.

Shep sniffed his friend. How much she'd changed since he met her. Not three suns ago, she'd been trembling on top of a grate Outside his window, afraid to jump down a distance not much larger than the one she'd just vaulted over. Now, she was bursting with confidence, joyfully commenting on the fact that she hadn't been crushed in her sleep. Something about the freedom of being without her girl, of running loose on the street — perhaps of meeting Frizzle? — had changed her into a new dog.

Frizzle. Just recalling the name sent shivers along Shep's fur. The bulldog had mostly been a pain in the tail, but he was brave and had kept the pack together when Shep had been sulking in the dark. If Shep had spent less time competing with the little yapper and more time thinking like a real rescuer, maybe Frizzle would still be alive. Maybe Shep would feel more like the leader everyone expected him to be.

The rest of their small pack was huddled near the trunk of a toppled tree in the bright light.

"Which way should we go?" woofed Cheese, his head tilted, curious.

Shep scanned the street. Both directions smelled of salt water — the kibble den was on a slight rise in the street, and on either side of it, farther downhill, Shep could see water from the wave still glinting over the pavement. The street itself was less street than garbage heap. Human things — boxes, papers, and shards of plastic, but also chairs, cabinets, and brightly colored cloths — were bunched up in mounds alongside the sand dunes and branches clogging the once open thoroughfare. A dead lizard rotted in the sunlight on a large metal box. A lonely red shoe floated upside down in a puddle.

The buildings along either side of the street were all in various states of destruction. One building looked unharmed, except for the ten-stretch-long metal stick sticking out of its side. The next was nothing more than a pile of stones studded with fins of wall — some decorated with patterns of flowers — and fangs of wood and plastic. A squat building with a tower like a snout sticking out of its roof slumped forward as if kneeling, its first floor having been washed completely away. Poles draped with loose metal strings leaned over the streets or were tangled in the trees' branches. A column of fire rose like orange breath from a metal pipe jutting out of a crushed den that was otherwise buried in mud.

Either direction led into a nightmare landscape. Shep glanced at Callie, who flicked her tail toward sunset.

"We go this way," Shep barked, and headed down the sunset side of the street.

CHAPTER 2
GARBAGE, GARBAGE EVERYWHERE, AND NOT A BITE TO EAT

As the pack wound its way through the jumble on the street, Shep began to scent just how much the wave had changed things. Every surface it had touched smelled of salt, and every puddle tasted salty and did nothing to quench a dog's thirst. The higher the sun rose and the hotter it got, the worse the problem became. By midsun, the pack was woozy from thirst and hunger.

Higgins licked his bushy furface to try to moisten his nose. "My snout," he whined, "I can't smell anything over the stench of salt and rot."

Rufus pawed at an overturned bucket. "We'll never find any food in this place," he grumbled. A shell with skinny legs and jagged pincer arms scrambled out from under the bucket and into the muck clogging a sewer grate.

"What was that?" Rufus cried.

Cheese loped to Rufus's side, then sniffed the grate. "That was a crab," he woofed as he lifted his long ears out of the tangle of leaves and trash. "They live at the beach. Why would a crab be here, away from the beach?"

"The wave smelled like the beach," barked Shep. "Maybe the crab came with the wave?"

Daisy shoved her stunted nose into the heap on the sewer grate. "Is a crab food?" she yapped.

"I'm not sure," woofed Cheese.

Daisy lifted her snout. "Then let's not — *snort* — waste time barking about it," she snapped. "If I don't get a bite of kibble soon, I'm going to get growly."

Like she's not already growling, Shep thought.

More strange creatures — alive and dead — littered the streets. A long, green-brown thing like the neck of Shep's family's floor-sucker slithered under a slab of stone. Something else that resembled a scaly human kibble-plate with eyes and a flat tail flopped in a shrinking puddle. Blue sacks of air, like blown-up poop bags, sat on tangled strings of jelly. Shep didn't want to try eating any of them — if they *looked* that odd, how good could they possibly *taste*?

The weirdness factor, however, only made Callie all the more curious. She trotted right up to one of the bags and gave it a lick.

"Ooh, Shep, it's salty!" she yipped, tail waving and ears

up. She hopped aside, offering a lick to any dog who wanted, and stepped on one of the jelly strings.

"And it bites!" cried Callie, leaping off the string. She desperately licked her paws to get them to stop stinging.

"Every dog!" Shep barked. "Back away from the poop bag!"

The pack startled. The dogs looked around their paws anxiously, searching for an attacking bag of poop, then began to scatter in different directions.

"What poop bag?" yipped Ginny, shuffling directly toward the thing.

"That blue balloon!" snapped Shep. But Ginny trundled directly onto the bag and caught her paws in the jelly strings.

"In Lassie's name, get it off me!" she yelped. Ginny stumbled back and tripped over Callie. The two girldogs rolled snout over tail into a mound of sand.

Shep couldn't help but pant as Ginny — all fluff and flailing paws — tried to right herself, and repeatedly smacked Callie in the snout.

"Would some dog offer a paw?" grumbled Callie as she winced away from Ginny's writhing rump.

Shep nudged Ginny with his muzzle and she got her paws under her.

"Let's agree that we'll stick to eating only the kibble we know," Shep woofed. "No more sampling of the poop bags, the scaly tubes, or anything that smells like the wave."

Oscar sank into a sagging sit. "But everything smells like the wave," he groaned.

"We'll find some fresh kibble, pup," Shep yipped, licking Oscar's head. *Great Wolf knows what we'll do if we don't. . . .*

Cheese swung his long snout up at the stone building across the street. "The wave didn't reach the rodent floor," he said. "Maybe the dens on the upper floors of that building stayed dry."

Higgins strutted to Cheese's side. "Could be worth checking," he barked. "Better that than stumbling around on poop bags that bite."

The dogs picked their way to the front of the squat building. Three rows of windows glinted on its face. The first level of the building had been drenched by the wave, but the upper levels seemed untouched.

Virgil snapped his teeth around the knob and, with one tug, pulled the entire door from the wall. He fell back, barely avoiding being crushed by the falling plank.

"What's wrong with the door?" he cried as he scrambled to his paws.

Callie sniffed the sodden door frame, which had buckled and broken from the single tug. "We have to be careful," she barked. "The whole world has changed. Things won't work the same as they did before the storm."

Shep nosed his way into the dark beyond the door. He stood in a dank hallway. The hall extended back into the building, and a staircase directly in front of him led up to the second level. Paper peeled back from the walls, curling down like giant leaves above him. Shep scented several distinct dens on the first floor, and more above.

"We need to find what kibble we can before the whole building collapses," Callie snuffled behind him. "Tell the pack to split up, small dogs with big."

Shep turned. "Higgins and Cheese, and Dover and Rufus, you cover this first level. There might be some food the wave missed. The rest, follow me and Callie up the stairs."

Boji pawed at the doorway. "Perhaps Oscar and I should wait here?" she woofed, tail waving hopefully.

"Smells good to me," Callie yipped. "You stay here and keep watch."

Boji's ears pricked up. "Watch? For what?"

"Anything," Shep woofed to her. "Everything." He licked Boji's snout and pawed Oscar's ear. "Bark and we'll all come running."

The second level was darker than the first, as the only light shone through one thin window in the building's front. Shep felt the building shiver when the wind gusted, and the floorboards groaned with the dogs' every step.

Shep split the teams up — Virgil with Ginny and Snoop with Daisy. Shep and Callie took the doors toward the back of the building; Shep figured that, as leaders, he and Callie should be brave and check out the dens farthest from the light.

As Shep and Callie moved into the shadows, they discovered that the back half of the hall had collapsed. Only one door was accessible, and it was already open, thanks to a large chair that was jammed into the door frame. Callie shoved her way under it to check the inside while Shep waited in the hall. The misplaced chair meant the wave had reached the upper levels, too. Shep's hopes sank — could any of the food have survived?

"The food room's been trashed," Callie said as she trotted out from under the chair.

Shep sniffed the pile of rubble that used to be the hall. "This stuff smells unstable. I don't think we can get to any other doors."

"Maybe we don't have to," Callie barked. She pawed at the wall, digging her claws into its surface. The paint crumbled and a small hole appeared. She scratched again, and a bigger chunk of wall fell out.

"Things don't work the same as before," woofed Callie, "but that's not always a bad thing."

Shep joined her in digging, and soon they had scratched a large hole through the wall to the den on the other side.

Callie squeezed her way into the den, and Shep stuck his head through the hole after her, flattening his ears to avoid a snarl of wires inside the wall. The den was dimly lit by windows along the opposite side of the room. The salt smell of the wave covered most surfaces, though Shep also scented fresh kibble, untouched by the salt.

Callie barked from farther inside the den, "The Bath room has fresh water in the big white bowl!" Shep heard a splash.

Desperate for a drink, Shep jerked his shoulders and wriggled his chest to fit through the hole. He tumbled into the den just as Callie emerged from the Bath room, muzzle moist with fresh water.

"There's kibble over that way," Shep woofed as he struggled to his paws. He raced to the Bath room and lapped up as much water as his stomach would bear.

When he was finished, he found Callie dragging a kibble bag across the floor. She spotted Shep and dropped the bag, panting with exhaustion.

"Good news — *pant* — the bag smells fresh," she managed. "But where's the dog who was supposed to eat it?"

Shep's tail drooped. He scented the air. "Not here," he woofed.

Callie slumped to her haunches. "How are we going to do this?" she sighed.

"Do what?" Shep woofed, padding over to his friend.

"Survive," she snuffled. "We haven't even been Outside for a full sun, and already we have stung paws, only one bowl of fresh water, and a single bag of kibble."

"I thought you found all this roof-falling-in-on-our-backs stuff exhilarating," Shep woofed, teasingly.

"That was before everything became so hard," Callie groaned.

Shep licked her nose and wagged his tail. "We'll think of something," he said, grinning. "Or, better yet, you'll think of something and I'll nose everyone into doing it."

Callie smiled. "Go team," she woofed in a goofy bark.

Shep dragged the kibble bag behind him as he and Callie climbed down the stairs. The others were waiting in front of the doorway, their tails wagging. A small pile of different kinds of human kibble rested on the collapsed entry door.

"Can you believe our luck?" yipped Rufus. "I smell cheese in one of the bags!" Drool dripped from his silver snout.

Callie nipped Shep's shoulder as he was about to step Outside.

"Drag the bag past Higgins," Callie snuffled, "and tell him to start dividing up the food."

"Why can't we all just dig in?" woofed Shep.

"Because if we do that, the dogs are going to stuff their snouts. There's not enough, even with this bag, to fill every dog's belly." Callie cocked her head as if waiting for Shep's thoughts to catch up with her own.

Shep looked at the kibble, then at the dogs. What Shep had considered a small pack suddenly seemed enormous.

"Okay," Shep groaned. "But why Higgins? I think I should divide the food. I am, after all, the big dog here."

Callie flapped her ears around her head, frustrated. "What do you know about how much kibble an Airedale needs versus a pug? A young pup versus an old timer?" Callie stood tall, but her ears drooped, like this was more barking than she thought necessary on the issue. "Higgins has done research on this stuff. He'll be fair."

Shep considered arguing with her, that Higgins was a bit of a tail dragger himself, but he didn't have any better ideas. And Higgins did know about breeds, a concept that Shep had a weak bite on at best.

Callie snorted impatiently. "I make the decisions on this team, right? So just follow my scent on this."

Shep was startled by her sharp tone. "Fine," he grumbled. "But Higgins better give me that old bone I see peeking out."

"You're the big dog, Shep," Callie woofed, flopping from the landing down onto the street, "not the Great Wolf accepting offerings."

Shep barked Callie's orders accordingly, first privately to Higgins, then to the whole pack. Higgins puffed up like a Ball at being given such an important job, and began at once calculating the rations each dog should get. Some dogs grumbled — Rufus (of course) and Ginny, who claimed to be on a special "high-fiber" diet — but Shep reminded them of what Callie had woofed, that this was a new world with new rules.

"One of those rules is that we share all our kibble, and it's divided fairly," Shep barked. "Don't worry," he said, somewhat more gently, "no dog's going to starve. We're all packmates."

They ate quietly in a tight ring of paws, each dog facing into the circle so that they looked at each other, and not at the wreckage of the world around them. Strange sounds reverberated off the buildings and streets. Bird cries carried from far away — or were they the shrieks of more buildings collapsing? As the clouds turned deep orange in the setting sun, every dog huddled closer into the circle.

CHAPTER 3
THE CASE FOR THE CAT

After eating, the dogs took turns running up the stairs to get a drink from the bowl Callie had sniffed out. Every dog was so parched, even Boji swallowed her fear and scrambled up the steps, eyes firmly shut until she reached the top.

Shep stood near the hole in the wall to direct every dog to the right place. Callie's snappish tone bothered him like a sore tooth — he just kept tonguing it, over and over. Yes, she was the thinker, but did that mean that he *couldn't* think? Was he allowed to make *any* decisions?

Virgil paused near a second staircase, which led up to the third level. "Did any dog check up there?" he woofed to Shep.

Shep loped to the stairs and gave them a sniff. "Doesn't smell like it."

. Virgil gave off an odor of nervousness.

That door almost crashing on his snout must've made him skittish. "I'll give it a quick scent," Shep yipped. "We can do a more thorough search in the morning if I catch a whiff of any kib."

Virgil smelled relieved. "I'll take up your post here until you return," he barked.

Decision made, Shep noted to himself.

He padded up the creaking steps. The third-floor hall was identical to the one below, dimly lit by the same front window, but now that it was evening and Shep was alone, the place seemed much spookier.

Shep sniffed the door frame at the top of the stairs, nearest the window. There was a strong scent of dog; one was either trapped inside the den, or had been until recently. The only problem was the splintered beam that lay between Shep and the knob.

Shep pressed the beam with his forepaw. The wood groaned, and sodden scraps of ceiling material dropped onto Shep's back. Then the whole section of wall — door and all — crumbled into the den with a crash.

Virgil barked up the stairs, "You all right?"

"I'm fine," woofed Shep, shaking flakes of wall from his snout. He coughed to clear the dust from his lungs, then sprang over the wreckage and into the den.

Everything inside smelled of salt from the wave. Mud lay thick on the floor. The dim light of the late sun filtered through the gauzy window cloths, which billowed out from broken windows. A moldering couch and cracked light-window stood at opposite ends of the room.

"Hello?" Shep woofed. "Is there a dog in here?"

A cat sprang from behind the couch, screeching like an old Car, and bolted down the den's dark hallway.

Shep sniffed the couch and confirmed that, at least before the storm, a dog had also lived in the den.

He loped into the den's food room to check if it was worth coming back up here for breakfast. It was not: the food room was a wreck. A mist of tiny flies hung over a bowl of rotting fruit on the counter. The cabinets had already been opened and scavenged, perhaps by the mangy cat. The room's outer wall had been torn away by the wave and the cold box had fallen through the floor. Shep stood on the lip of floor that remained and looked down at his packmates, who'd gathered in the street.

It struck Shep that this was the first time since he'd left his den that he found himself alone. Only the creaking of the building and the whisper of his own breath tickled his ears. The quiet felt strange, though only a few suns before, Shep had lived a solitary life with his boy. How quickly his mind had adjusted to the constant bark and banter of the pack. Then again, Shep was used to radical changes — he'd gone from fighter to wild dog to pet, from the safety of his boy's room to the violent chaos of the storm.

Shep sighed. He'd better check the remaining rooms to

smell if the dog had survived, then join the others before it was completely dark.

"Fuzz said we had a visitor."

A golden girldog stood in the doorway to the den's main room. Her wispy fur was matted in places, but Shep could tell that in better times, she'd been well cared for. The scrawny cat he'd seen before sat on her back.

The girldog padded closer, her fluffy tail flapping. "You smell like a nice dog," she woofed. "I'm Honey!"

"Who's Fuzz?" Shep asked, wagging his tail.

"Fuzz is Fuzz," the cat spat in a sort of half meow, half bark.

The fur nearly sprang from Shep's back. *The cat speaks dog!* "You taught him to bark?" Shep snapped at the girldog.

"Fuzz is my friend," Honey woofed. "I know it's not supposed to be done, but I wanted to bark with him, so I taught him a few woofs. He taught himself the rest." She grinned and waved her tail.

Shep sniffed the girldog, scenting for crazy. She'd violated the most basic code: A dog never spoke to another species, not ever. Dogs barked with dogs. Anything else was like woofing to your kibble: a sign you were four paws in the hole and going under.

Why did Honey even want to bark with the bony thing? Shep could smell maybe woofing to a fine hunting cat, but this meower looked heartbeats away from splintering like a cracked window. The cat had been hit by the storm harder than the girldog. His black fur was so matted it stuck to his

24

skin. His spine stood like a line of hackles along his back, and his hip and shoulder bones jutted up like small ears.

"Well, I'm Shep," he said finally, "and I'm here to help you." He explained about the others, about how they'd survived the storm.

Honey listened, becoming excited as Shep barked, her tail wagging harder and harder. "Oh, Fuzzle!" she woofed. "We're saved, just like I told you!"

"How go with Shep-dog and he friends mean we saved?" the cat hissed. "You have food, Shep-dog? You have safe den to sleep?" The cat's strange eyes — glowing green orbs split with black, as if torn by a claw — glared at Shep.

Shep did not address the cat; he spoke only to Honey. "I won't force you to come," he said, "but you might be safer with other dogs, safe from wild dogs and the like. I can't promise anything, though."

Honey panted gently. "Don't mind Fuzzle," she woofed, glancing back at the cat and licking him on the nose. "He's a worrier. We'd love to join your pack."

We? "Sorry," Shep woofed, "no cats."

"Why not?" Honey asked, her head tilting.

This girldog was looking at him like he was the crazy one, but clearly she was the one who'd grown fur on her brain. "He's a *cat*," Shep barked. "A cat can't be a part of a pack of dogs."

Honey's tail drooped. "Then I can't go with you. Fuzz is declawed, defenseless. I'm his only hope until our family returns."

"Well, declawed or not, he can't be in my pack." Shep glanced down through the floor-hole at his friends. "We're tight on food as it is. No one's going to want to share his kibble with a cat."

"If that's how you feel, then I don't even *want* to be a part of your pack." Honey's tail stood high and her proud eyes glared into Shep's own, unafraid and unwavering.

The cat licked his paw, flashing Shep a scathing look. "Some dog have honor, like Honey-friend. You, Shep-dog, no honor."

Shep growled as he considered things. Here was a big decision, and Callie wasn't around to make it. *That's good*, thought Shep. *This will show her that I can be a decider, too.*

He couldn't leave a dog alone in a wrecked den with no kibble, he just couldn't, not after everything he'd been through. But the pack would never accept a cat. *Right?* Cats were . . . well, not dogs. They were Others; they were strange and solitary and smelled funny. Shep had sometimes watched strays in the alley below his den, hissing and spitting and scratching and screeching — cats were weird, simple as that.

But this was one cat. A defenseless cat in need of help. And he was a scrawny thing; maybe no one would notice him.

"Fine," Shep sighed. "The cat can come, too."

Shep hesitated in the doorway. The street shimmered with heat, though the sun was low in the sky and the moon already shone like a ghost near sunrise. He smelled the pack in the alley toward sunset.

"What are you waiting for?" Honey woofed, sticking her head Out beside Shep's.

"Shep-dog waiting to see if maybe Fuzz get eaten by snake before meet dog-pack." The cat hissed at Shep from his perch on Honey's back.

Why couldn't Fuzz have been a nice cat, a friendly cat, a cat that didn't make you want to bite his bony neck in half? There might have been some chance of convincing the others with a nice cat. With Fuzz, Shep just hoped Callie didn't eat him before he and Honey could scramble back to their den.

In the alley, the pack was moaning about sleeping arrangements.

"Are we sleeping Outside?" whined Oscar. "I don't think I can sleep Outside. Those poop bags could use their jelly strings to strangle me in my sleep!" His tail was set firmly between his legs.

"Don't be silly, pup," barked Ginny. "No dog of my breeding sleeps Outside like a common mutt." She stood and shook her fur. "Where *are* we sleeping?" she woofed to Shep as he approached. "And don't say this tottering pile of stones." She flicked her muzzle at Honey's building.

Virgil shifted on his paws. "I agree," he grunted. "And I don't advise we start sniffing around in another building in the dark." He then lowered his head. "If you'd like my opinion, Shep."

"What about the yard?" woofed Honey, stepping out of the shadows. "There's a little Park behind my building with a stone fence around it. We'd be Outside, but the fence might protect us from a poop bag with jelly strings. What *is* a poop bag with jelly strings, anyway? Sounds exciting!"

She trotted into the group, panting happily, her tail wagging, but no one looked at her — everyone stared at the cat.

Higgins coughed slightly. "Uh, miss, uh, golden mix? Yes?"

"Goldendoodle! Isn't that fun? I'm Honey the Goldendoodle! I just love my name." She flashed her bright eyes at each dog.

"Yes, dear," Higgins yapped, "but have you noticed that there's a cat sitting on your withers?"

Honey panted. "Oh, yes," she woofed. "That's Fuzz. He's a Maine coon cat. Say hello, Fuzz!"

"Hello, dog-pack," Fuzz hiss-barked.

Every single jaw and tail dropped.

"Did that cat just bark?" Daisy yipped out the side of her jowl.

Shep stepped forward. *Time to assert some big dog authority.*

"Yes," he woofed, "the cat barks. And he's joining our pack."

Jaws remained open, but now all eyes were on Shep. Callie flicked her tail to the side, indicating she wanted a private woof with him, but he ignored her. *I'm a decider,* Shep reminded himself.

"Fuzz is Honey's friend, and a special cat, as you can smell." Shep licked his jowls. "He's — well, first, he can bark. Which is unusual."

"Unusual?" yapped Ginny. "By Lassie's golden coat, it's undogly!"

Shep stood taller. "Unusual or not, he can bark, and we can understand him, which is kind of interesting, in addition to being undogly, right?" He panted lightly, looking each dog in the snout. Cheese waved his tail, and then Boji did. Dover licked his nose. Callie remained still as a rawhide chewie, eyes wide and tail low.

Shep continued, "And he can catch mice, which will help with the food problem." He glanced at Honey, who had a dubious expression on her muzzle. The pack caught whiff of Honey's uncertainty, and tails began to fall again.

Shep reasserted his stance, chest out and tail high, ears up. "He's a pet who needs our help," he barked, loud and clear. "Why should Fuzz be treated differently than any dog we find? Are we going to turn away a pet who asks for help, even if it's not a pet we'd want under other circumstances? I don't think that's the kind of pack we are. This storm has left all kinds in need of help, and if we happen to be the ones who can help them, then I think we *should* help them."

Oscar leapt at Shep's paws. "Yeah!" he bayed. "This is what it means to be the Great Wolf! Shep even stands up for stinking cats."

The other dogs remained still. Honey grinned, her mouth

open in a friendly pant, and she waved her tail. Fuzz grimaced, ears back, ready to bolt. Shep wasn't sure if he should remain strong or loosen up and wag his tail.

Dover licked his jowls. "Honey, did you say something about a yard?"

"Yes!" Shep bayed, a little too loudly. "Let's all head to the yard!"

"Okay," Honey woofed, somewhat confused. "Follow me." She trotted past Shep.

"Let's move!" snapped Shep.

The dogs — out of bewilderment? Because Shep told them to? — followed Honey down the narrow alley along the side of her building. At the back of the building was a stone wall, as she'd woofed. A metal gate hung off the wall, ripped from its fastenings by the wave. Shep swiped it with a paw and the gate clattered to the ground. The pack filed into the yard, glancing warily at Shep as they passed.

The yard was only a few stretches wide, and was littered with odd bits of trash from the storm, but one corner was sheltered by a fat, old banyan tree. Its massive trunk was surrounded by a cage of roots, which grew down from the tree's low, spreading branches. Some had walls of bark between the rope of root and the trunk, forming miniature dens within the shadows.

"It's perfect," Oscar woofed, marveling.

Shep watched as the pack wound its way into the sheltered dark and snuggled close to the trunk. Callie appeared at his side.

"Bold move," she woofed, her bark cold.

"I'm sorry I didn't bark with you about the cat," Shep replied, "but I thought I'd lose the pack if I stepped aside."

"I just wish you'd woofed about this rescue idea with me beforehand. I'm all for saving dogs, but now we're supposed to rescue *all* the animals we find?"

"Not all," Shep snuffled, "just those we can help."

"Which ones are those, Shep?" Callie yapped. "Are you going to make calls on whether we have anything to offer a particular ferret who squeaks for assistance? We're barely surviving as it is!" Her eyes were hard.

"Honey wouldn't come without him," Shep barked. "I didn't want to leave her behind, and I figured it's one cat, and he can bark, which makes him special, right?" Callie's eyes seemed to be softening. He woofed on, "We don't have to rescue every pet we come across. I mean, how many rodents speak dog? I'm guessing none."

Callie hung her head. "I'm not really angry about that," she grumbled. "I know what you meant. But you didn't say that — you said *every* pet who needs our help. As lead dog, you have to say only what you mean, only what you're willing to fight for with all the fur on your back."

"How do you know what a lead dog can and can't say?" Shep growled. "All you ever do is hide behind my flank."

Callie scowled, her jaw locked and ears flat against her head. "That was mean," she snuffled.

Shep sighed. Why was she making this so difficult? "I'm sorry," he grumbled. "I had to make a call up there, so I made one. I'm trying my best, Callie."

"Aren't we all," she woofed, and padded away from him into the darkness of the banyan's roots.

CHAPTER 4
NEW FRIENDS, OLD ENEMIES

Three suns had passed since the pack left the kibble den, and they'd spent that time moving from building to pile of rubble to building, searching for food and water and other dogs trapped by the storm. It was slow and difficult work, as they had to watch out for unstable floors and ceilings, collapsing walls, and vents of foul-smelling air that burst into flame if a dog flicked his tail at them the wrong way. The pack only cleared one or two buildings in a sun, collecting scraps of kibble, snoutfuls of water, and a few dogs, though too often they found only casualties of the wave. When the Silver Moon appeared, they would gather under the banyan tree.

Shep sat in the shadow of the tree watching fat clouds burn orange and pink in the setting sun. His whiskers twitched, sensing the dropping air pressure — rain was coming. The first drop splashed on his snout. *Guess it's already here.*

The rest of the pack trickled in a few dogs at a time, returning to the old banyan tree for the night. Though the dogs had once fit comfortably beneath its sprawling branches, there were now too many in the group. Dogs lay hunched against one another, legs on snouts, paws in jowls.

Shep spotted Fuzz on one of the lower branches, staring down at him with a look of pure disgust, as if Shep was to blame for the crowding, the rain, everything. The pack had mostly ignored the cat, and Fuzz made a point of keeping out of every dog's way. Every dog, that is, except Shep. Fuzz materialized like a malevolent hairball every place Shep went. Shep was sniffing out a wrecked den — "Shep-dog miss food packet in book room" was hissed from a corner. Shep took one stinking heartbeat to tug on a sock with another mutt — "Shep-dog think it wise to take fun-break while dog-pack starve?" It was like having a foul-tongued flea chattering in his ear.

It didn't help that Honey was always following Shep around, asking him about his life before the storm or offering him some special piece of kibble she found. Shep would have to bark with her in the morning about getting the cat — and herself — out of his fur. He had no idea what he'd woof (how do you tell a nice girldog to go sniff some other tree?), but he had to get the cat off his tail.

Callie trotted to Shep's side. "Five more dogs this sun. That puts us over twenty."

"The cat's always watching me," Shep grumbled. "No matter where I go, those green eyes follow." He squinted at Fuzz's silhouette amidst the leaves.

"I don't know where we're going to put them all," Callie woofed.

"Didn't I *save* the stinking meower?" Shep snuffled. "Shouldn't he be grateful?" He looked down at Callie as if noticing her for the first time. "Were you just woofing at me?"

She flicked her snout up at him. "What?" she asked. "Oh, yes," she yipped. "We're going to need to sniff out a new den."

"We just need to rearrange a few dogs," Shep barked. The thought of trying to move such a large pack through this city of deadly traps smelled like a three-sun-old squirrel carcass — bad, bad, bad.

A sharp squeak pierced the soft murmur of the pack.

"Please remove your snout from my fur," growled Ginny to an oversized newcomer, a Bernese something or other named Hulk.

"Maybe you should keep your fur from frizzing in my muzzle," Hulk snarled.

Ginny snorted with surprise, then flashed a look at Shep like he should stick his snout into their scuffle. When he made no move to intervene, Ginny thrust out her chest defiantly.

"Lassie would never allow a mutt to growl at a ladydog like that!" She tucked her paws up into her belly and buried her muzzle in her fluff.

Callie had a told-you-so smirk on her snout. "Still think we can solve things with a little reorganization?"

Shep forced his tail up — he smelled that Callie was looking for a fight.

"I don't disagree with you," he said. "I just think we might be sniffing up the Black Dog's rump to move this many dogs anywhere."

"Black Dog's rump or no, we have to find a den with more room." Callie nosed her way under a large plastic sheet that lay over the space between two heaps of trash, then yipped for Shep to follow.

Shep glanced up at the clouds, which had expanded and now covered the sky like a gray blanket. He winced at the raindrops, then shuffled under the tarp after Callie. He had to crouch to fit under the flimsy roof, and rain dripped on his scruff through a hole. Callie curled near his head against a mud-stained pink stuffed rabbit.

Callie continued, her woofs muffled by the rabbit's puff tail. "It's like when there are too few toys in the Park. All the dogs tear each other's fur out to get their teeth on the one bone." She snapped her jaws around the rabbit's tail and growled, curly tail wagging. She tugged the tuft and the whole toy fell on her head. Callie rolled with the rabbit, growling and kicking her paws and wagging her tail — in a heartbeat, she'd become that carefree pup Shep had met on the balcony. It felt like cycles ago, though it was really only a biteful of suns.

"I think you killed it," Shep woofed as Callie reduced the rabbit to a pile of stuffing.

"Huh?" she yipped, ears and tail up, a tuft of fluff caught on her fang. She snorted a pant. "Right," she barked, smiling. "Where was I?" She pushed the toy under her paws. And, suddenly, she was back to being the serious, pushy yapper the storm had created. "My point is that with every dog piled on top of one another, we won't have to worry about 'if' there will be a fight. There will definitely be a fight, the only question is how many suns we have till it happens. Then you'll have to break it up, and the loser will think you were unfair and challenge you, and the last thing this pack needs is a power struggle." She barked like she'd been running dog packs all her life. "We only have us dogs to rely on — no girls, no boys. Every dog needs to know who's in charge of keeping her safe."

Shep watched Callie, her features a deeper black in the all-consuming blackness of the cloudy, moonless night. Ever since the storm, no human lights had glowed in the city. Once the sun was gone, there was only moonlight or no light at all.

He didn't disagree with her woofs. What itched Shep's ear was that *he* wasn't quite sure who was in charge of this pack. Callie said that "they" were the pack's leaders, but she made him bark only her orders, and never even asked his opinion about things. *What am I?* he grumbled. *Just a bigger snout for her to bark out of?*

He growled at himself for thinking such a rotten thing about his friend. Callie had always stuck by him. They were a team. And she was good at ideas, the thinking stuff. Shep had thoroughly botched his last decision; he needed to stick to being the doer. He was good at the doing. This was their thing, him and Callie. It worked.

Shep woke to a bleak gray dawn. His fur was soaked and his tongue felt coated in grit.

Callie hopped to her paws and stretched. "We'd better sniff out a new den before sunset," she woofed. "You snored in my snout all night!" She grinned and wagged her tail — she must have forgiven Shep.

Shep howled to wake the pack, then barked that they were moving on to a larger den.

"Where are we pawing to?" woofed Virgil, loping to Shep's side.

"We'll find out by sundown," he replied quietly.

Virgil gave a curt nod of his snout, then began barking and nipping the raggedy pack into some semblance of order — small and old dogs in the center, larger and fitter dogs surrounding them for protection.

As the sun blazed across its arc overhead, the pack moved down the street. Shep barked for teams of dogs to sniff out each building that they passed. The rest of the pack snuffled around in the garbage clogging the gutters until all the scouts returned.

"Find anything?" woofed Callie as Shep loped out of a new-looking metal-and-glass building.

"Water came in through the vents in the walls and ceiling," he wheezed, "but the windows held so the air's stale and thick with mold." He snorted to clear his nose of the stench. "You find any kib? I'm starved."

"I got a candy wrapper with some crumbs stuck to it and a can that's been punctured, take your pick."

Shep's jowls curled at the offering. "What's in the can?" he groaned.

"Mystery juice." Callie nosed the can over to him and started licking the wrapper. "It's nutty," she woofed, ears drooping. "I hate nuts."

The juice leaking out of the can tasted like sugar-coated rotten fruit — disgusting. "You can have this, too," Shep grunted, rolling the can with his nose toward Callie.

A little brown and white mutt named Waffle, a pointer mix according to Higgins, dragged a tree branch out of a rubble pile near the gutter.

"Whoa!" he barked. "I've got the biggest stick!"

He tried to lift the whole branch in his mouth, but could barely drag it along by one end. A tan pitbull named Paulie was on the dragging end of the branch in a heartbeat. He wrapped his jaws around it and began a tug-of-war with Waffle. Soon, a number of dogs were in on the game — every dog loves Big Stick. Boji lugged a huge plastic tube from a pile and Hulk, Cheese, and Snoop chased her around the trash heaps.

Callie scrambled onto a box, tail waving and ears up, watching for an opening to jump into the game. "What are you waiting for?" she woofed to Shep.

What am *I waiting for?* Shep wondered. The answer came to him in a heartbeat. *I'm waiting for my boy.*

Shep used to play Big Stick with his boy at the dog beach. He would find the most ludicrous pieces of driftwood — drift-trees, to be accurate — and carry them over to the boy. The boy would laugh and try to tug the stick from Shep's locked jaws. Shep always ended up tackling the boy, both of them getting coated in sand, the stick long forgotten.

The happy yips and barks of his packmates echoed throughout the empty street. Shep had never felt so alone.

A breeze whistled between two buildings toward Shep. It carried a strange scent. Dog, but not pet. A scent laced with dried lifeblood, filth, and now the salt scent of the wave.

Wild dogs.

"Every dog!" Shep bayed. "Head for sunset!"

The game halted — Waffle and Paulie dropped their stick; Boji paused and looked at him, white tube protruding from her jaws. They seemed confused. Then Virgil caught the scent.

"Wild dogs!" he howled.

Those dogs who'd been in the kibble den wheeled on their paws and pounded down the pavement. The new rescues tilted their heads.

"What's the hurry?" woofed Hulk.

The first wild dog — a mottled brown and black mutt —

skulked out of an alley near sunrise. "I thought I scented a gaggle of pets," the wild dog snarled, "fresh for the feasting." He growled, jowls trembling, then dove at a little black and white mop of hair named Baxter.

"Run, you fur-brains!" Shep bellowed.

He sprang over a plastic bin and tackled the wild dog before he could latch on to the yapper. The fluffy guy was scared out of his fur. A huge, tree bark brown mastiff girldog named Mooch snatched Baxter in her jaws and dashed down the street toward sunset.

The wild dog rolled Shep into a stone wall. "Your pack's left you, pet," he snapped. "Ready to be my next meal?"

Shep got his paws under him and hauled himself into a defensive stance, tail to the wall. "Maybe you remember me?" he barked. "I'm the pet who killed your leader, Kaz."

Recognition flashed across the wild dog's muzzle. "All the more reason to relish gnawing the marrow from your bones."

The wild dog snapped at Shep's jowl. Shep feinted toward the dog's ear, but then ducked, turning his head and scraping the flesh of the dog's shoulder. Shep rolled on his back and thrust his paws into the dog's ribs, launching him into the wall. The dog hit the stone and flopped onto the ground; unconscious or dead, Shep didn't care.

A howl reverberated from farther down the alley — more wild dogs. The scent of battle was a treat to them: One whiff and they came running from all directions. This was Shep's heartbeat to escape.

He sprang to his paws and raced toward sunset.

"Ha-roo, Shep! You were amazing!" Oscar's squeaky howl pierced the silence of the street.

Shep whirled and saw the silly pup on top of a crushed Car. Shep scrambled back toward Oscar, the scent of wild dog growing stronger. Shep could hear their rasping breaths.

"Are you positively out of your *fur*?" he barked at the pup.

Oscar cowered. "I just wanted to see you fight again," he whimpered.

Shep didn't bother arguing with the crazy yapper. He snapped Oscar into his jaws and bolted down the street after the rest of the pack.

CHAPTER 5
THE CROSSING

Shep zigzagged down the trash-strewn street, Oscar dangling from his jaws. The pup seemed to be having the time of his life. He kept howling with joy, "I'm in a real chase!" like there weren't Great Wolf knows how many wild dogs on their tails. Shep prayed that the pup's skin wouldn't split on his fangs.

The large buildings along the street's edge gave way to smaller structures, many of which had been flattened by the storm. Only a wall or two of most survived. Shep sprang onto a toppled tree and saw his pack gathered not far from where he stood. *Why did they stop?* he wondered, leaping down from the trunk. As he approached, the pets parted, and he saw the problem at paw.

The road ended at a wide, brackish river at least fifteen

stretches across, like a street of water. On its surface was a scum of refuse, and whole tree trunks whirled in the water's flow. A ramp in the stone wall holding the river led down from the street to a narrow dock. On the other side of the river, there was another dock attached to a staircase that led up the opposite side to the street.

Callie was perched on the wall at the water's edge, yapping with Higgins and Daisy. Shep dropped Oscar at Boji's side.

"Wait, Shep!" the pup cried. "Can't I go with you?"

"Stay with Boji!" he barked, maybe a little too sharply. He saw the pup wince, then whimper, but he had no time to apologize. He bounded to Callie's side.

"Why have you stopped?" he woofed. "There's a pack of wild dogs on our scent."

"You've noticed perhaps the gigantic river that cuts through the road?" she replied.

"It's not a river," yipped Higgins. "It's a canal. Humans cross them on boats, but there aren't any boats at the dock."

"We'll swim it," Shep barked. "As a bonus, the water might cover our scent."

"Not all dogs can swim," growled Daisy, who looked about as buoyant as a stone.

Honey stuck her nose into the conversation. "Fuzz and I know a way to get you across, Daisy," she woofed.

"Yes," hissed the cat. "Dog swim on dog. Fuzz and Honey-friend show." He nipped Honey's ear and she dutifully raced down the ramp and leapt into the water. She paddled across with Fuzz sitting on her back, then pulled herself out on the other side.

"Brilliant!" barked Callie, but the rest of the dogs began to anxiously lick their jaws or chatter their teeth.

"I don't care if I have to haul every dog into that canal by the scruff," snapped Shep. "You get your tails into that water!"

Shep scented their fear — the pack seemed unsure whether they were more afraid of him or the wild dogs. *That's not good*, he thought. He didn't want his own pack afraid of him.

He loped up to Oscar, who sulked against Boji's hind leg. "You want to be a hero, pup?"

Oscar was on his paws in a heartbeat, tail whipping back and forth. "I'll do anything for you, Shep!" he yipped.

"Follow me," Shep barked.

Shep padded down the ramp, with Oscar scrambling after, then dove into the water. He swam next to the dock so Oscar could climb on his back. The pup did so, trembling from nose to tail, but with a brave grin on his jowls. As soon as Oscar was settled on Shep's withers, Shep paddled out into the river.

"It's working!" barked Higgins. "The stinking cat was right!"

Shep glanced back at the rest of the dogs and was relieved to see that they were following him. Cheese bounded down the ramp and leapt into the water like he was born to swim. Hulk gingerly dipped his paw into the canal, then belly flopped into the water. Poor Baxter, who was still a bundle of trembles from the wild dog's attack, trundled onto Hulk's back and they began floating across the water.

Honey and Fuzz cheered the dogs on from the opposite dock.

"It's easy!" Honey barked. "Just go for it!"

"Yes, fat-dog," spat Fuzz. "You look like good float for fluffy-fur."

Hulk stopped near Shep with a jerk, nearly knocking Baxter from his perch. "I felt something!" he squealed.

Shep sniffed the water. "It's probably just one of those little flickery things that swim in water," he barked, recalling the tank in the kibble den. "Just keep going!"

The dogs' splashes rang up and down the walls of the canal. Some small dogs, like Callie, chugged along with the big dogs through the water. Shep kept glancing over his shoulder at the street, praying that every dog made it in before the wild pack caught up with them.

"Ouch!" yelped a big brown dog, Bernie — a Rhodesian ridgeback (Shep liked that name). "Something just nicked my paw!"

"Keep paddling!" Callie barked.

"Keep those paws pumping!" Oscar yapped from Shep's back.

The first dogs reached the other side and Honey helped to pull them from the water.

"Help!" yapped Daisy. Her paws scraped at Dover's fur as she slipped from his back.

Cheese paddled to her side and nosed her back up onto Dover's withers. "There you g —"

Cheese disappeared under the water.

"Cheese!" Daisy cried, nearly plunging in behind him.

"Hold on!" barked Dover, paddling with all his strength.

Shep couldn't do anything with Oscar on his back. He dug his paws through the water as fast as he could. Some of the dogs already on the dock dove back into the canal. Virgil was the first to reach where Cheese had been.

"Nothing!" Virgil snapped. "Just bubbles from below!"

Suddenly, the water churned. Something the size of a tree rolled near the surface. Bubbles foamed around the violently thrashing form. Terrified, Shep drifted, paws still. The rest of the pack stalled, too, and watched the raging water.

Dover pulled himself onto the dock. "Everyone, out of the water!" he cried. *"Get out now!"* His bark was frantic, like his very life depended on every dog being on the dock with him.

Shep shook off his fear and repeated Dover's command. "Dig, dogs! Dig in!"

The water calmed — the tree-monster was gone. All that remained was a froth of scum on the canal's surface. But Shep scented a new danger.

"Thought you'd shaken us, pets?"

The wild pack had finally caught up with them. The first wild dog to the edge of the river jumped right in with a crash. Shep spotted a tree branch glide out of a nearby eddy. The branch split into a mouth of sharp teeth and snapped around the wild dog. The dog barely had time to yelp before being dragged underwater and rolled by the tree.

Shep dug his claws through the river as fast as he could until he reached the dock. He pulled himself onto it, dripping and panting hard with Oscar still clinging to his fur like a tick.

The wild pack stayed on the opposite side of the water, watching the lifeblood of their packmate stain the canal's roiling surface. There were only a few wild dogs in this pack — nothing like what Shep had fought in the kibble den.

"Catch you next sun," snapped one girldog. The wild dogs scattered into the shadows.

The second tree stopped rolling and sank into the dark water. Shep noticed that the other trees in the canal were moving against the current.

They weren't trees — they were all alive.

Callie sniffed the edge of the dock, then looked at Dover. "Do you know what happened to Cheese?" Every few heartbeats, a violent tremble rippled over her body.

Dover stared across the black water. "Water lizard," he woofed quietly. "Humans call them Gators. I've done some swamp hunting with my master. He always shied away from any place he saw a water lizard."

"Can we kill it?" Virgil growled. "Can we save Cheese?" His jaws were set tight.

"No," Dover said. "Water lizards are big — some as long as a Car. There was nothing any of us could do to save Cheese."

The shoulders of Shep's packmates pressed against him — the dock groaned under their collective weight. All eyes watched the canal's flowing surface as if the water itself threatened to swirl into a giant mouth and suck them all down. They were terrified, and that meant they were easy pickings for any predator, be it wild dog or monster tree. Shep had to distract them. Get them moving. That was his job as the doer.

"Every dog!" he barked. "Up the stairs to the street!" He nipped the rumps and shoulders of the dogs nearest him, and the pack began to move.

"Time to walk on your own four paws," Shep woofed to Oscar. He lay down and the pup slid onto the dock.

Honey shoved through the crowd of dogs, her tail low. "I'm so sorry, Shep!" she cried. "I wish I'd kept my snout shut about swimming. But I promise I didn't know about the water lizards."

"Why are you sorry?" woofed Shep. "I'm the one who ordered every dog into the canal."

"See, Honey-friend?" spat Fuzz, who crept out from under Honey's belly. "This not Honey-friend's fault, so stop with the sad-tail. Everything Shep-dog fault." Fuzz shot Shep a defiant look, as if daring Shep to disagree with his assessment.

The clouds began to drip — the pack needed to find a place to hole up for the night. Shep swallowed his pride and straightened his stance. "The cat's right," he woofed. "This is on my withers. You had a good idea." Shep licked Honey's snout.

Honey's tail waved and a shy grin spread across her jowls. "It was Fuzz's idea, too," she yipped.

Fuzz licked a paw and ran it over his ears. "Fuzz no expect thanks from Shep-dog," he hissed.

Oscar puffed out his little chest and strutted up to the meower. "Hey, furball, who do you think you're hissing at?" he growled. "If it weren't for Shep, this pack would've eaten —"

Shep nipped Oscar on the scruff. "Let's just get off this dock, okay?" he woofed.

Oscar snorted at the cat and trotted over to the staircase, which of course he couldn't climb, so he stood there, glaring at the step, until Shep lifted him in his jaws and carried him up to the street. Fuzz flicked the pup in the nose with his ridiculously long, fluffy tail as he passed them on the stairs.

Callie was waiting for Shep at the top of the steps. "This is bad," she groaned. "It's raining, and we were just attacked by trees with teeth, and the whole pack is twitchy watching for wild dogs and water lizards."

Shep dropped Oscar, then lifted his head so he was snout-to-snout with Callie. "Breathe," he woofed. "First thing, we need to get away from this river of death and find someplace to sleep before we're all soaked to the skin."

Callie took a deep breath in, then snorted. "Ugh!" she yipped. "Snoutful of Shep breath!"

Shep found Virgil, and the two of them barked the pack into some order so that they could move away from the canal. They allowed Boji a last mournful look at the water, which rippled with raindrops. When it became clear that she was staying in her sit, Shep padded to her side.

"I can't leave him," Boji woofed.

"And I can't leave you here, Boji," Shep snuffled. "The pack needs you. Who else is going to keep those evil steps in check?" He smiled at her and she waved her tail.

"Could you say something?" she said. "Like you did for Frizzle? Cheese so admired you. It would mean a lot to him. And to me."

Shep looked into her deep brown eyes — how could he say no to her? But he was no good at this. What he'd said for Frizzle had been a fluke; the woofs burbled up from the horrible guilt he'd felt. He couldn't have yapped a bark if he'd really *thought* about it. However, looking at Boji's muzzle, he sensed she wasn't leaving without his saying something.

Shep faced the canal. "Cheese — grr, Wensleydale, you

always had a wag in your tail and a grin on your snout. You were there for your packmates when they needed you. With your last pant, you were helping a friend. I hope we can all say the same when the Great Wolf comes for us."

Boji smiled and bowed her head. "Thank you," she woofed. She gave the murky waters one last look, then stood. "I'm ready now."

They turned, and the whole pack was facing them, every dog standing tall. As Shep passed through them, they wagged their tails. They didn't smell afraid anymore.

Shep found Callie near the front of the group.

"I don't know where you come up with this stuff," she woofed, "but you really have a gift." She licked his snout.

It was nearly dark as the pack moved down the street, away from the canal, toward sunset. They hadn't gone far when Shep spotted a huge black box. As he moved closer, he saw that it was one of those long Cars that Shep's boy used to call a "bus." This bus was tipped on its side and its front window was broken, but otherwise it looked solid — like the Silver Moon had left a cave in the middle of the street for a bedraggled pack of dogs to curl up in.

"Come here!" Shep howled over the patter of rain on the trash.

The bus was jammed against a small stone building. Shep padded alongside the building, out of the rain, to give him a clearer scent of the area. His nose only registered the rain until he sniffed inside the bus. Then, a strong smell of dog and rot reached his nose.

Great Wolf, no . . .

Eyes sparkled in the darkness. *A wild dog?*

"This is my den," a girldog growled. "Get out or get fanged."

CHAPTER 6
BLAZE

Shep stepped back, not wanting to start a fight with a wild dog in such a tight space. The girldog crept forward, her head low and fangs bared. The faint light's flicker in her eyes and on her wet nose gave Shep a sense of her size: smaller than him, but not by much.

"I said *out*," she growled.

"We're not here to start trouble," Shep woofed, his bark calm but firm. He kept his tail and head high. He did not want to show any submissiveness to the girldog.

The girldog glanced behind Shep at the others, barely visible in the evening's shadows. She sniffed the air. "You smell like pets," she woofed. "Wet pets."

"We *are* pets," Callie yipped. "And we'd like to get out of this rain."

"Who's the yapper?" the girldog snapped.

"That's Callie, and I'm Shep," Shep woofed. "We need a safe den for the night and were hoping to sleep here." He waved his snout into the dark recesses of the bus. "Smells like there's room enough for all."

The girldog glared at them for a few more heartbeats, then snorted. "You can sleep here tonight," she grumbled. "But you'll have to clear out come sunrise." She loped along the floor, which had been the windowed side of the bus, and disappeared behind the half wall created by the last row of seats.

"Quite rude," Higgins yapped. "She's a Queensland heeler, and a pet like the rest of us, I'd bet my tail on it. No need to be all huffy." He scampered into the bus and flopped down on a mound of fabric.

The others padded timidly into the bus, wary of the small, dark space. The roof was a row of windows; the rain drummed on the glass, creating a thundering roar inside the metal walls. Some dogs curled in the spaces between the rows of seats, but most huddled in clumps near the front of the bus and anxiously scanned the dark streets.

Shep loped to the back, near where he'd seen the girldog disappear. He found her curled up against the floor-wall, snout on her paws.

"What?" she grunted. "I need my rest."

"Don't get growly," Shep woofed. "I just came to smell if you were all right."

The girldog panted. "Oh, are you going to be my big

protector?" she moaned. "Well, you're four suns too late," she snapped. "I've learned to protect myself."

Shep flattened his ears. Why was he barking with this girldog, who was clearly a tail dragger? Then again, she smelled like grass and sunshine and human hands, like the very best sun at the Park.

"You mind moving, hero?" she grunted. "You're drooling on my snout."

Shep licked his teeth, trying to scrape his tongue clean so he could bark a witty retort, something that would make him look less like a drooly, fur-brained mutt with two paws in the hole.

He dropped onto his haunches and flicked his ears forward. "I'm more than a protector," he snuffled. "I'm a door opener, kibble finder, and endlessly yapping snout in your ear."

The girldog lifted her head. "A full-service pain in the tail if I've ever smelled one," she said. Shep could tell from her bark that she was grinning.

The girldog pushed herself up into a sit. The faint light silhouetted her lovely tall, pointed ears and long, tapering snout. Her short fur was a mottled gray-black that reminded Shep of the Great Wolf's silvery coat. Her muzzle was a mix of black and brown with a slash of white cutting from above one eye, along her snout, and under her jaw. When she turned her head, the cloud-dimmed moonlight shone in her eyes, and Shep saw that one was bright blue and the other brown.

"So, how did you come to lead this pack of misfit pets?" she woofed.

"I, uh, well," Shep sputtered, still gazing into her eyes.

"You, uh, well, what?" she barked, cocking her head and smiling.

"We all just sort of came together," Shep managed, "for protection." His mouth felt dry; his barks were all wrong again. "You could join us," he yipped. "If you wanted to. I mean, I smell you've been doing pretty well on your own. Right?"

She stood and her snout was a whisker-length from Shep's own. All he could smell was her scent and it was rich as lifeblood. Her warm breath misted on his nose.

"Not so well that I wouldn't mind some company." She licked his jowl; her touch sent shivers down to his toes.

"I'll join your pack," she woofed. She flicked her snout toward where the others were piled in the shadows. "Looks like you could use another real dog to balance out all those yappers."

Shep's tail wagged in circles, though he tried to keep a serious look on his muzzle. "Well, that'd be very good. I mean, good. I mean, I'm glad to have you." He licked his jowls.

"You can call me Blaze."

"Blaze," he sighed.

She curled back up on the floor, grinning. "Good night, Shepherd."

"Shepherd," he sighed, standing. "I mean, good night."

Shep stumbled over sleeping dogs as he made his way toward the front of the bus. He felt dizzy and fur-brained and needed a sniff of fresh air. He also figured some dog should keep a watch out for water lizards or anything else that might surface in the night. Just as he was about to stick his snout through the shattered front window of the bus, Callie strutted out of the shadows.

"Where were you?" she yapped.

"I went to check out the rest of the bus," he woofed nervously, though he didn't know why he felt so nervous. "And to scent out that girldog."

"So that's why you're all slobber-tongued."

"I'm not slobber-tongued," Shep protested, though even he could sense how silly he sounded. "I mean, I thought I should give her a smell, make sure she isn't wild, you know?"

"Really?" Callie's brown eyes were like noses sniffing his thoughts.

"She's a very nice girldog, in fact," Shep continued, barks pouring from his jowls like drool, "not wild at all, and I asked her to join our pack, and she said yes."

"She called me a yapper," Callie snapped.

"I'll tell her to stop saying that, if it bothers you," Shep woofed.

"It doesn't matter if she *stops* saying it. She's already barked it! It's already out there, stinking up the whole den." Callie was yapping loudly. Dogs were lifting their heads and staring.

Callie was nearly frothing at the mouth. "In sum," she snarled, "I don't like her." She panted loudly.

Callie didn't smell like her usual reasonable self. Shep tilted his head. "You sure that's what's itching you?" he asked.

"What, that's not a good enough reason for you? You think that's nothing, calling some dog a yapper?"

"I just think —"

"Well, don't think," Callie snapped. "*I* know. Calling me a yapper is as good as calling me a mutt."

"What's so bad about calling a dog a mutt?" Shep woofed.

Callie dropped her snout and looked at the floor. "Only a purebred could woof that."

Shep crouched in front of Callie and gave her a quick lick on the jowl. "Callie, every dog in this pack thinks you're made of bacon. Especially me. We'd have lost the Great Wolf's scent a long time ago without you."

Callie looked at Shep. "I hope you tell the new dog that," she woofed. "She called me a yapper to make me feel unimportant, worthless. To show the pack — to show *you* that she was better than me."

"I'm sure she doesn't think that," Shep woofed, not at all sure that Blaze didn't think of Callie as just another dog. Shep knew he should tell Blaze that Callie was the real leader of the pack, but then Blaze would know that Shep was only the doer, the snout out of which Callie barked. He didn't want Blaze to see him that way. He wanted to be her hero.

Callie limply scratched at her ear. "Just remember what I said back at the tree: The last thing this pack needs is a power struggle. And that dog smells like she thinks she's the alpha, not you and me." She retreated into the dark of the bus and sank into sleep.

Shep sat at the front of the bus and looked out the window at the sky. A steady rain fell from a sheet of cloud. The city was as dark as Shep had ever seen it, with only the faintest light shining through the clouds from the hidden moon high above. He wished he could see the Great Wolf's sparkling coat; he needed guidance. How could he lead as a team with Callie and not have Blaze think less of him? But he didn't want to lead without Callie. He also didn't want to kick Blaze out of the pack. Everything was so difficult in this storm-wrecked world.

Shep wondered, as he had every night since the storm, if his boy was somewhere in this darkness, looking up at the same cloud-cluttered sky. He hoped not. Shep didn't want to be trapped in this ruined place; he wouldn't wish such a fate on any dog. But at least he'd been trained to survive in the fight cage; at least he was toughened to the harsh things of the world. His boy was as soft as a new pup. He wouldn't last a sun on the streets of the drowned city.

As if answering Shep's thoughts, a howl echoed through the dark. If he hadn't seen him washed away in the wave, Shep would've sworn it was Zeus's call.

The first tails of dawn woke Shep from his slumber. He'd dreamt of the river of dogs again, only this time it was he who was drowning. He'd looked up and seen the endless stream of pounding paws. He'd barked for help, but not one dog had glanced down as he sank deeper and deeper.

He lapped at a foul-tasting puddle of rainwater Outside the broken window of the bus, then scanned the surrounding street. Both sides were lined with stone buildings, some a few floors tall, all in various states of destruction. He wondered if the pack shouldn't split up and scrounge for scraps in smaller groups — they might have better luck looking in more than one place. *We'd be easier prey for any attacker. Then again, with strange things like water lizards around, are any of us safe, even in a pack?*

Callie woofed in her sleep, her tiny paws twitching. He wondered what she was dreaming about and hoped it was a happy dream. He would hunt up some kibble for her, to make up for their spat. *Maybe I'll catch her a squirrel*, he thought, though the idea made him gag.

Blaze hopped over Snoop's sleeping form and joined Shep on the street. "You're the first pet I've encountered who wakes before midsun," she barked. "Look at the rest of them," she yipped, waving her snout at the bus. "Lazy as the cycle is long."

"Why are you all proud-snouted?" Shep woofed. "You're a pet like the rest of us."

Blaze swiped at a pile of rubble. "You and I are not like *them*," she woofed. A chunk of stone tumbled out of the pile, revealing a cache of hidden kibble. Blaze waved her tail. "Want a bite?"

Shep scented jerky treats in Blaze's stash. Slaver cascaded from his jowls. "Maybe just a nibble," he yipped.

"So why don't you tell me your story?" barked Blaze.

Shep wondered what story to tell. Begin in the fight cage? Would that be too horrible? Begin with the storm, with meeting Callie? *Was that where my life began?*

"Where were you born?" Blaze prompted.

"I was born in a kennel," Shep answered. "Now you."

"Me, too," she barked.

"And?" he asked.

"And?" she repeated mockingly.

Shep whipped around and leapt at her chest, toppling her into a puddle.

"Ha!" she snapped. "Fight dog, right?"

Shep was surprised — impressed? — that Blaze could divine this information from a single attack. But the excited look on her muzzle made him nervous.

"Yes," he grunted, "I was born in a fight kennel."

"Don't be shy," Blaze yipped, slapping the dirt, her tail and rump waving behind her. "It's nice to meet a dog who hasn't had his life handed to him in a silver bowl."

Shep stepped back, away from Blaze, cutting off their play. "The fight kennel never handed me anything except a cage," Shep barked flatly. "You wouldn't understand."

Blaze stood, tail lower but still wagging. She slinked closer to Shep, rubbing his flank. "This is a tough world, and you're a tough dog. Why are you ashamed of it?"

"I'm not ashamed," Shep woofed, wondering what she meant, whether he *was* ashamed. "And what's so tough about your world? You look like a pet who's seen her share of comfy beds and bowls piled with kibble." He sounded a bit more defensive than he'd meant to.

"Now look who's barking about things he knows nothing about." Blaze trotted away from the bus, toward the canal. She paused and looked back over her long tail at Shep. "You coming, hero?"

Shep glanced at the bus full of snoozing pets. He should stay and guard them. But he could go with Blaze just for a few heartbeats, maybe hunt up some kibble, and no dog would notice. *Right?*

He saw Blaze's marbled coat shimmer in the morning light. "I'm coming!" he barked.

As they snuffled through the jumble on the street, supposedly scenting for food, Blaze told Shep about her past. She was born in a kennel inland, near a big lake filled with water lizards. She was taken from her litter by a young man in a wide-brimmed brown hat. He started to whistle and talk to her, and fed her scraps of dried meat. It took a few suns, but she soon understood that with each whistle he wanted her to sit, or stop, or walk toward him, to lie down at his paws or jump at a toy in his hands.

After a moon-cycle of work, the man took Blaze to a

fat building with a curved roof, which oozed the acrid stench of manure and was surrounded by endless fields broken up by long stretches of fencing. It was hot and humid, like her kennel had been, but the only life in this place was the huge, snorting brown beasts. They groaned and grunted in the fat building, and tromped lazily through the open grasses. Blaze knew that she was the alpha of these creatures, though they were a full stretch taller than she was, and longer and wider by more, outweighing her like a Car to a yapper.

She barked at the young man to let her at the beasts, that she knew she could beat them; instead, the man walked her around the whole property, letting her sniff the new smells. The next sun, he put her in a pen with a few of the massive creatures. Blaze scampered up to them, but the beasts didn't move. She wanted them to move, needed them to move so she could collect them for her man, show him that she knew she was these creatures' master. She sniffed at the paw of one of the animals. The beasts' fur ended in a cloven, bony toe, so Blaze nipped at the tender skin just above that horny bit. The beast gave a snort, then lumbered a step forward. Success!

The man then whistled at her, and she remembered that the whistle — high, two blasts — meant to run to one side of the man. He whistled like that again, and Blaze nipped the beasts to move to that side. The man leapt to his feet and fed her a treat. He went through each of the whistles he'd taught her, and Blaze realized that they were never meant to direct her, but to tell her what to do with the fat, snorty beasts.

The man made her practice on the few beasts in the pen for two more suns. Each evening, Blaze lay on the porch of the man's den and looked out at the masses of beasts in the fields, longing to try her skills on such a test.

On the third sun, he took her out into the open grassland. Racing with the beasts, driving them first one way, then the other, staring down charging strays — it was like discovering that the fur she'd always worn was a mere blanket covering the fiery stuff beneath. Lifeblood pounded through her, and she slept each night the dreamless sleep of a happy dog.

There were a few other dogs working on the big herds, and they accepted Blaze as a partner. They were never a pack — each dog kept to herself. But they were friendly enough, and good workers. Some of the men kept dogs other than their herding dogs. Those men would put the other dogs in an empty stall at night to make them fight. Those fight dogs were kept apart from Blaze and her partners.

"It sounded like the end of the world sometimes, listening to those fights," Blaze snuffled.

Shep knew exactly what she meant.

"So how did you end up here?" Shep woofed.

Blaze panted, grinning. "My man came here a few suns before the storm to visit his kin," she yipped. "Funny how a chance thing like taking a vacation can lead to such a disaster."

The winds had howled as loud as the big-wheeled farm machines. The gusts clattered the glass in the windows. Blaze's man and his kin huddled in the dark around the kitchen table, where several candles flickered. There was a pounding at the door; Blaze barked fiercely at the noise. She scented that her man was anxious, and that the knocking only made him more upset.

The man answered the door, holding Blaze back by her collar. Several strangers dressed in green uniforms burst into the room and began shouting commands. The man yelled at the strangers, clutching Blaze to his chest, and the strangers yelled back. Blaze barked and snapped at one of the green men. Something changed after that. She was dragged by one of the strangers in green away from her man and locked in the Bath room. The door was opened a few heartbeats later and a bag of kibble was tossed inside. She heard her man shouting, then the rumble of footsteps and the slam of the door, and then only the wind.

Blaze smelled the air shifting; she knew she had to get out of that den and rescue her man. She broke the door to the room she'd been trapped in, then smashed through a window to escape. She roamed the streets sniffing for her man, but couldn't pick up his scent. When the winds became unbearable, she found shelter under a boxy den near the canal. Then she smelled a strange salt scent in the air — the wave.

She ducked out from under the den and saw the water rising in the canal. A Car lay on its back near the building she'd hidden under. Blaze climbed onto the Car, and scrambled onto the den-building's roof. The winds tore at her fur, and the rain soaked her, and she knew that she clung to her life by a claw. Then the wave smashed into the den beneath her and flattened it. The roof, however, floated on top of the water in a single piece. Blaze rode the roof like a boat until it smashed into a stone wall on the other side of the canal. She clambered onto that stone building and waited until the water washed away.

"After the wave, I tried to keep moving, but that fire inside me had been blown out by the storm." She licked her jowls and sighed. "I'll never find my man, never get to smell my home or my partners and the beasts again." She pawed a sheet of rusted metal and a shiny cockroach skittered out of a puddle and under another piece of trash. "All I have left is this wasteland full of scuttling things."

Shep licked her nose. "And me," he woofed.

Blaze licked his nose back. "And your pack of yappers," she yipped.

"*Our* pack of yappers," he barked.

CHAPTER 7
SHELTER

Shep and Blaze headed back toward the bus. As they loped through the scattered buildings and piles of rubble, Shep told Blaze his story: about the fight kennel, about rescuing the dogs, about the fight at the kibble den, and finally about how much he missed his boy.

"I'd give my front paw to smell my boy again," Shep woofed.

"I feel like I lost my front paw when the green strangers took my man from me," Blaze said, sighing.

They went on about their humans, what they were like and the silly things they did, like wearing shoes and watching the light-window. It made Shep happy to tell Blaze all about his boy, and to hear about her man. The only other dog he really barked with was Callie, and she only ever woofed about the stuff of this world, the world of the storm, the world without people.

By the time they turned onto the street where the bus lay, it was midsun and the pack was scattered, sniffing around in the trash. Callie was furious — her hackles were up and her tail was low.

"And where have you been, *partner*?" she grumbled.

"What are you, his master?" snapped Blaze. "We were out. Hunting."

Callie trembled with rage. "I'm not his master," she snarled, trying very hard to keep her bark even. "We're a *team*. And teammates don't run off for half a sun without leaving some whiff of where they went."

Shep stuck his snout between the two before the fur started to fly. "You're right," he woofed to Callie. "I should have woken you." Callie's hackles smoothed, but Blaze sneered. Shep continued, "Anyway, looks like everything's well-furred here."

Callie's tail started to wag. "Yes, things are good here, no thanks to you," she woofed. "Virgil and Honey scavenged one of the surrounding buildings and found a whole loaf of bread in one of the dens. We saved you each a slice." She snagged two pieces of bread from inside the bus's broken front window and dropped them at Shep's paws.

Callie straightened her stance. "This den smells like the perfect haven to wait in for the humans to return," she barked loudly, as if trying to catch the attention of all the nearby dogs. "We're close to buildings to scavenge, we're safe from the rain, and with only one entrance, we can defend it easily. Now that you're a part of the pack, Blaze, I'm sure you won't mind if we all share your den." Callie glared defiantly into Blaze's muzzle.

"Clever dog," Blaze snuffled, a rather frightening smile spreading over her jowls. "Of course, you all are welcome to share this den," she barked, matching Callie's strident tone. "But I don't recommend it. This bus is not as safe as it looks. There's a hole somewhere in the back that rats can get through. And one way in means one way out: We're too easy to trap."

Shep felt like something important was going on, but he hadn't the faintest scent of what it was. It smelled like Callie and Blaze were having a marking contest, only no dog was peeing.

Callie stepped closer to Blaze. "So you'd have us wander the streets looking for someplace slightly safer, all the while leaving us prey to whatever wants to attack us, be it a wild dog or a water lizard?"

"No need to wander," Blaze barked. "I know the perfect place." And with that, she turned tail and shot off down an alley.

"Virgil!" Callie bayed. "You're in charge. Higgins, follow me!" Then she raced after Blaze.

Shep felt like the odd dog out. Should he follow or stay? He wanted to follow. Callie had left Virgil in charge. *I'm following*, he concluded and charged down the alley. He tracked the fresh scent of Callie's chase — she reeked of anger — and soon caught up with the three of them.

They stood before a wider section of canal, almost the size of the Park. The twisted remains of docks floated in the water. On the sunset side of the canal, the stone wall was smoothed to form a steep ramp up to street level. The space around the ramp was open pavement, edged by trees and grass, and then low buildings — or would have been, save for the pack of various-sized boats cluttering the plaza. The alpha of these seafaring survivors lay on its side several stretches from the top of the ramp, jammed against the buildings: a giant boat, thirty stretches long at least.

"It's sturdy," Blaze woofed, "and all the walls and floors are intact, even if some of the windows are broken. It's a lot more than one dog can defend, but I think the pack of us can keep it secure."

Shep stared. His boy had taken him on a boat once, though one much smaller than the specimen lying on the street in front of him. Shep hadn't liked riding in that boat. It had bounced around on the water and spat spray at him as it skittered along the waves. But this boat looked calm enough, sleeping on its side. Perhaps when out of the water, boats couldn't give a dog stomach cramps that made him moan for a whole sun.

If that was true, it was perfect in every way. The boat looked big enough to house the whole pack, with extra space for any other dogs they rescued. The top level was smashed, but below it was a level lined with windows, and Shep thought there was another level still inside the curved beetle-shell of the boat's hull: The part of the boat that cut through the water was a single sheet of plastic save for a band of small windows like eyes around its edge.

In terms of defense, the boat appeared impenetrable. Its topmost level was pressed against a building, its hull was solid, and the space between the curve of the beetle-bottom and the street was jammed full of sand and garbage. That left only the narrow, square back and pointed front, and the windowed top-side exposed. Any attackers would have a tough time finding a way in.

Even better, all around them were buildings to be scavenged for food. And finding a drink wouldn't be a problem, as several of the small boats in the plaza were filled with fresh rainwater. It was paradise!

"My, my," woofed Higgins, "now that's a yacht if I ever smelled one."

"It's not a yacht," barked Shep. "It's a boat."

Higgins growled, then snorted loudly. "A yacht *is* a boat, you fuzz head."

"Watch it, Furface," Blaze grumbled, moving to stand over Higgins.

Surprise flashed across Higgins's muzzle, but he left it alone. Shep panted to himself — it was nice to have one dog on his side. Then again, did he need Blaze to defend him? And from Higgins, at that? Higgins was just joking. *Right?*

"If we can stay on the scent," Callie snapped. "How do we get inside this thing?"

The dogs loped closer to the top level of the boat, which was crushed against the metal-covered front of one of the buildings. The plastic sheets and metal branches that had once formed flimsy walls on this upper deck were bent and folded against the building, forming a web of ceiling. Dim shafts of light shone through the bars, illuminating the tangle of wreckage on the street. About ten stretches in, the cracked remains of a window wall extended above a wide counter with a silver wheel, which Shep recognized as the place humans sat to control the boat.

Higgins sniffed the metal front of the building. "Smells salty," he yapped. "The wave must've knocked the boat out of the canal and rammed it into this wall."

Callie poked her nose into the debris. "There's a hole in the boat's wall — grr, former floor, it seems. I think it leads into the den." She leapt over a toppled stool and trotted straight up to the edge of the hole, gave a quick sniff, then glanced back at the others, ears up and tail waving. "Last dog in is a soggy kibble!" she barked and sprang into the dark.

Blaze snorted, as if offended by Callie's exuberance, then bounded in after her. Higgins scampered through the hole and got stuck halfway through. Shep nudged his rump, pushing him inside. The Furface glanced back, and in a sheepish woof, said, "Much obliged."

73

"Oblige taken," Shep replied, feeling like he'd regained the better bite.

Higgins looked confused for a heartbeat, then snorted and pranced into the dark.

The hole led from the crushed floor into a fancy den, which was maybe four stretches tall, but only two wide. The ceiling and the back wall were entirely made up of tinted windows. The bronze light filtered down to reveal overturned furniture — couches and chairs, all with shiny patterned fabric cushions, and small tables surrounded by broken human stuff. The floor beneath Shep's paws was a wall of windows that matched the ceiling. Some were cracked, but the floor was otherwise solid — no fear of intruders from below.

Toward the front of the boat was a section of wall that ended a stretch up from the floor. Blaze hooked her paws onto the edge of the wall, then pulled herself up onto a landing. "There are more rooms down here," she barked, sniffing the air. "And I smell kibble." She took a step, tumbled forward, and disappeared.

"Blaze!" Shep cried, bounding to the half wall and springing onto it. He nearly knocked snouts with Blaze, who was dragging herself up out of a wide hole.

"I found the kibble," she groaned, pulling her rump onto the landing.

"You okay?" Shep whimpered, tail low. "What's that hole doing in the floor?"

"It's a door," grumbled Higgins. He'd made a ramp from the fancy den to the raised landing out of a cushion.

"Remember, the boat is on its side, so there will be doors in the floor and in the ceiling." He took a step toward the door-hole and his paw slipped on a strip of plastic. Suddenly, lights blazed throughout the narrow room, which was revealed to be a short hallway. There was a second hole in the floor a stretch farther down the hall, and a matching hole in the ceiling, its door dangling open like a tongue from a jowl. At the end of the hall were two other doors, both closed.

"We have lights?" yipped Callie as she sprang into the hall.

"Appears so," answered Higgins. He slid his paw along the strip and the light went away.

"Hey!" barked Shep.

The lights flicked on again.

"My snout, this little strip turns the lights on *and* off!" Higgins excitedly shuffled his paw back and forth along the strip, clicking the lights on and off.

"Enough!" bayed Blaze.

Higgins froze, leaving the lights on. He was panting, his eyes wide and furface abristle. "Sorry," he woofed, giving a curt snort and regaining composure. "Got a bit carried away. Never knew how these things worked. Always exciting to make a new discovery, eh?" He wagged his stub of a tail, growling happily as he sniffed the little strip.

The others seemed to feel as unnerved as Shep was from all the flashing. Callie gave an all-over shake.

"How about we leave the lights off?" she woofed, sliding her paw over the strip and clicking them back into the dark. "I've gotten used to no lights."

"I agree," barked Blaze, who recovered her composure with a swift lick of her jowls. "We have to keep it dark." She leapt over the floor-hole, and stretched up on her hind legs to inspect the door-hole in the ceiling. "If we're the only thing in this city with lights, we're going to attract a lot of unwanted guests." She gripped the edge of the door-hole with her forepaws and, with a little jump, pulled herself through it into the room above.

"I thought vermin liked to hide in the dark," Callie barked, a snarky whine to her voice.

Blaze stuck her head down through the ceiling-hole. "I'm not barking about vermin," she snapped. "I'm barking about wild dogs."

Blaze explained that she'd run into some wild dogs during the storm. "A big, black girldog," Blaze woofed. "I didn't like the lay of her fur."

The memory of Kaz's huge body slumped in a pool of her own lifeblood blinded Shep for a heartbeat.

"You don't have to bother about her," barked Higgins. "Shep defeated her in a devilish fierce scrap."

Shep's vision cleared and caught Blaze's stare — a mix of awe and ownership.

"That's my Shepherd," she woofed, then ducked back up into the room above.

Callie grimaced at the door-hole in the ceiling, a low growl rumbling from her muzzle.

The holes in the floor led into a narrow food room. Shep

opened all the cabinets, and Higgins set about figuring out how much edible kibble they'd stumbled upon. Shep left Higgins piling packets of food and pulled himself up into the hallway, then through the door-hole into the ceiling room.

The ceiling-hole led into what had once been a food-eating room. It had a windowed ceiling and the end of the room closest to the rear of the boat was open to the main, fancy den. Blaze was in the process of shoving a long wooden table toward that opening. She jammed her shoulder into the table's leg and the table tottered, then slid down into the fancy den. The bottom of the table landed with a crash on a toppled sofa, but the end nearest Shep leaned against the floor of the ceiling room.

"What did you do that for?" Shep woofed.

Callie answered his question. "Okay, great! Now the chairs!" she bellowed from the main den.

"She's a pushy little yapper," Blaze said to Shep, "but her brain's kicking with all four paws."

Shep helped Blaze drag the chairs to the edge of the opening, and Blaze explained Callie's plans. "She thought of using the table as a ramp, so that the smaller dogs could get up here. I haven't the foggiest scent of what she's doing with the chairs."

Once Shep and Blaze shoved the chairs down, Callie nosed them together to make a more sturdy ramp than Higgins's cushion from the main den up the half-wall into the hallway.

"That's a well-furred idea if I've ever smelled one," woofed Blaze as she marveled at Callie's engineering.

Callie's tail wagged at the compliment — almost, it seemed, against her will.

Both doors at the end of the hall were easily defeated — they had the best kinds of knobs: the flat, slappable kind. The first door opened into a large room that tapered to a point — the front of the boat. There was a gigantic human bed-cushion splayed on the curved floor (which had been the wall when the boat was upright). The floor and ceiling were inset with small, tinted windows. Just above the entry door was another door. Shep and Blaze piled pillows into a ramp to get up to it and found that the door opened into a tiny Bath room, complete with working water paws. Because the boat was on its side, the water paws and bowls were an easy stretch from the floor; even Callie could swat them and get a slurp of water.

"I claim this room for Shep!" barked Blaze. "He's the alpha, so he gets the best den."

Just as Shep was about the mark the door frame, Callie snorted her disapproval.

"What does he need this huge space for?" she yapped. "No, this big den should be for dams and pups, or sick dogs." She sniffed the giant mattress and pawed at the overstuffed pillows strewn around it. "Yes, this will be a perfect, quiet, dark den for them."

Shep whimpered softly — he'd liked the idea of himself,

and perhaps Blaze, curled up on that giant bed — but he knew Callie was right. "This is a perfect sick den," he woofed, loping back into the hallway.

Blaze followed him out of the room. "Who's the alpha of this pack again?" she snarled.

The other door at the end of the hall, which was in the floor, opened into an enclosed stairwell. One set of stairs led to the crushed level.

"A second exit," woofed Blaze.

"A second entry to defend," grumbled Shep.

The other staircase led deeper into the boat, to the curved beetle-bottom of the hull.

The bottom level of the boat was dark as the Black Dog's hide. Shep and Blaze pushed open the door from the stairwell and hooked their paws onto the wall, which was now the floor. Shep's claws scraped one of Higgins's plastic strips. When clicked, the lights illuminated a narrow hall lined with three doors each in the ceiling and floor, and one door in the wall at the back end of the boat. That door opened into a huge, dark room crowded with pipes and smelling of chemicals and grease, like a pack of Cars was huddled inside. The other rooms — some a few stretches long, others barely a stretch — contained human bed-cushions and little Bath rooms, also with functioning water paws. Each room had one or two small, Higgins-sized windows.

Higgins decided that one of the small rooms near the front of the boat on the bottom level would be good as a kibble storage room. "I'll be able to keep better track of what's going in and out if I'm not amidst the hubbub of the main den." Shep, Callie, and Blaze helped him to drag the kibble from the boat's food room to the designated storage room.

When they had finished moving the food, Callie gave the bottom deck of the boat a once-over sniff. "The big dogs will stay on this level," she woofed. "The small on the main level, in that big fancy room."

"No good," barked Blaze. "Then you yappers will be exposed to attack. I say we build ramps into and out of the dens on the lower level for the small and sick and old, and keep the working and fighting dogs closer to the entry points."

Callie glared at Shep. "I thought you were going to woof with her about the whole 'yapper' issue?"

Shep sighed. "Blaze, Callie doesn't like the word 'yapper.' Please don't bark it anymore."

"Fine," yipped Blaze, like this was a ridiculous request. "What do you want to be called?"

Callie seemed flustered by Blaze's reaction. "Well, small dogs, or just dogs." Callie regained her defensive stance. "And what's this about working dogs? You don't think small dogs can work?"

Shep stuck his nose between the two girldogs. "Do we have to get our hackles up about everything?" he woofed. "Can't we just take each other's barks with a bite of kibble? At least pretend to get along? For this sun?"

Both the girldogs dropped their tails and smoothed their hackles.

"You're right," yipped Callie. "I'm sorry."

"Well," barked Blaze. "So long as that's settled. Let's build some ramps."

"Shep!" whined Callie.

Shep sighed. This was not going to work, having to negotiate every woof between Blaze and Callie. "Why don't I go back and get the rest of the pack? You two stay here and sort yourselves out."

He turned tail and navigated the maze of holes through the boat before either of them could argue with him. As he stepped Out from the main den onto the crushed floor, he saw Blaze emerge from the stairwell's exit. She picked her way across the debris; Shep waited.

"I told the yapper — Callie — that she could organize the den however she wanted," Blaze woofed. "I don't want to push you away." She touched her nose to Shep's, and he felt that tingle ripple under his fur.

"Callie has good ideas," Shep said, trying to stay focused. "You said so yourself."

Blaze stepped over a piece of plastic that separated her from Shep. "You're right," she yipped. "And she is smart." Her mismatched eyes sparkled in the golden, late midsun light. "I sense there's something between you two." Blaze brushed past him and stepped out onto the plaza.

"She's my best friend," barked Shep, joining her. "We've been through a lot together."

"Well, so long as she's just a friend," Blaze woofed, sidling up to Shep's flank.

He licked Blaze's snout. "Callie and I have made a good team," he said. "She's the brains, and I'm the muscle."

"Don't underestimate yourself," barked Blaze. "You've got a good share of both."

CHAPTER 8
CLAWING UP THE
LEARNING CURVE

Blaze returned to the boat to help Callie and Higgins set up the den, while Shep ran back to the bus to lead the dogs to their new home. The pack moved easily into the huge spaces of the boat. The big dogs scratched together their dens on the bottom level in the rooms that had to be climbed into or out of. The small dogs all made their dens in the large main room. Boji took up residence with the two pregnant dams in the big bed room to help them whelp their litters when the time came.

The pets were most excited about the lights. Higgins had turned them on to make it easier for every dog to find their way around, and as a kind of celebration for their first night in the new den.

"I haven't seen a light since my family left me!" cried Rosie, a shaggy, black papillon mutt with wild hairs sprouting from her pointy ears. She seemed about ready to burst out of her fur with joy.

"There was a light just this shade of goldenrod in my den's Bath room," whimpered Ginny.

"I hate to piddle on every dog's patch," yapped Higgins, "but I haven't the foggiest idea as to why the lights in the boat are functioning when the rest of the blasted city's dark as a cat's soul — pardon the expression, Fuzz."

Fuzz spat something snarly in cat-speak, then replied in his meow-bark, "Fuzz no take offense, dog-with-hair-for-nose."

Higgins's furface bristled, but he continued, "In sum, I don't think we should waste whatever light we have."

"I agree with the small hairy dog," woofed Blaze.

"Higgins," snapped Callie.

"Right," said Blaze. "Higgins. If we leave the lights on, we're inviting every dog in the city to attack."

"Don't we want to attract lost dogs?" yipped Honey.

"Not all dogs are lost," growled Blaze. "You should remember that before some wild dog returns your sweet little welcome with a fang to the jowl."

Honey couldn't have looked more shocked if Blaze had actually fanged her in the muzzle.

Shep nosed his way to the center of the pack. "Okay! So we'll all leave the lights off unless there's an emergency."

"Except the light in the bottom level's hall," snuffled Callie.

"Except the light in the bottom level's hall!" repeated Shep.

The dogs dug into the cushions and nosed the odds and ends left in the boat into individual dens. Toppled couches became comfortable caves; pillows were piled together to make luxurious nests. As the sky flamed deep orange, Higgins barked that kibble distribution would begin on the lower level.

In a heartbeat, dogs crowded the narrow stairwell, worried that the first snout to the kibble room would get the biggest share. Shep had been helping a bunch of tiny brown and gray dogs turn a broken chair into a bed and was now caught in the main den by the snarl in the stairwell. He ran up the table-ramp into the ceiling room, then dropped down onto the crowd shoving to get into the door leading to the stairs.

"Stop pushing!" he howled. "Every dog will get his share!"

Virgil caught Shep's scent and barked from where he stood, jammed in the stairwell. "Form a line!" he bayed. "Against the wall, you mangy mutts!"

Shep heard Daisy's snorty woof from inside the main den. "You heard Shep — *snort* — get in line!"

The mass of rippling fur began to settle out into a line of dogs. *Thank the Great Wolf,* thought Shep. He would bark with Callie about coming up with a better plan for mealtimes.

Oscar wriggled from between the bushy legs of a large, hairy black dog — a Newtie? Noofle? — and scampered up to Shep.

"Hey!" Oscar yipped like he hadn't smelled Shep in suns. "I barked with Callie about my sharing a den with you and the other big dogs, but she said I should stay in the main den. Could you woof with her and change her mind?" He whipped his thin tail in circles.

Shep licked his jowls. *How to let the pup down easy . . .*

"Well, Oscar," Shep began, "I'm actually with Callie on this one. I'm in a den on the ceiling with Blaze, and —"

"Oh," Oscar grumbled. "So you already have a denmate?" His tail and ears sagged.

"Yeah," Shep woofed, feeling rotten for not even thinking that Oscar might have wanted to share his den.

The pup straightened his tail and pricked his ears. "That's okay," he yipped. "I met this other pup, Odie, and he offered to share his cushion. Maybe the three of us can play later?"

Shep was distracted by a sharp bark.

"You took an extra kibble!"

"Did not!"

"I smelled it! You took two brown lumps, not the one we're allowed!"

"My snout! Calm down!" yapped Higgins.

Shep thought he recognized one of the voices, but they both sounded angry.

"Shep?" Oscar whined. "Can you play later?"

"What?" Shep replied, shaking his snout. "Sorry, Oscar, but I'd better get to the kibble room."

Shep pushed his way through the mob in the stairwell, then lunged over the other dogs' backs to get to the lower level. As he pushed through the door-hole, he saw ahead of him what was quickly becoming a frenzy.

Two dogs were tearing into one another, fangs and claws slashing. Around those two, several other dogs were snapping at each other, but most were barking at Higgins to give them their food. Higgins stood in front of the kibble, tiny chest out and fangs bared, daring any of the scoundrels to pounce. The remaining dogs were paralyzed with fear, and some chattered their teeth or whimpered.

Shep shoved past the last few dogs and leapt into the fight. He grabbed the larger of the two by the scruff and threw her into the wall. The smaller dog froze, then cowered.

The girldog — who must've been a new rescue, as Shep had never smelled her before — snapped to her paws. "Who're you?" she growled. "And where's my second kibble?"

Shep laid his ears back and bared his fangs. "I'm the alpha of this den," he snarled, "which means I have the final say on everything, including kibble."

The girldog squinted her eyes, as if considering whether or not to challenge Shep. Shep quickly took in the details of the space — low ceiling, wider floor with den holes breaking through every few stretches, and dogs blocking every escape.

It'd be a tough fight, but winnable, though perhaps at the cost of an innocent dog's lifeblood.

The girldog dropped her tail and lay down at Shep's paws. "I didn't mean to start a fight," she grumbled. "But the old yapper took two kibbles. The hairy-faced yapper said we could only each have one."

Shep stood tall and glared down at the cowering yapper. "Did you take an extra kibble?"

It was Rufus, the cursed tail dragger. He was trembling uncontrollably. "I-I-I was so hungry, Shep," he whimpered. "And this den is so dark and small. I didn't think any dog would notice."

Shep lowered his head so he could look directly into the yapper's beady black eyes. "I notice *everything*," he growled.

Rufus trembled even harder and began wailing deliriously. He rolled onto his back, exposing his bare white belly.

Shep felt the eyes of every dog in the pack on his fur. Great Wolf, how he wished Callie could simply appear beside him and whisper what to do next. *What would the Great Wolf do?* he wondered, remembering Callie's words to him.

Rufus was powerless, and obviously terrified out of his fur, so there was little point in attacking him further. The girldog had been right that Rufus had taken more than his share, but that didn't excuse her starting a fight, especially with a dog less than half her size. The rest of the dogs needed to understand that if they had a problem, they had to solve it without fighting. They had to come to him, as the dogs of old came to the Great Wolf.

Shep lifted his head and raised his ears and tail. He opened his throat to give the loudest and deepest bark he could make. He looked first at the girldog. "You're new here," he began, "so you don't know our rules. But to clarify for every dog, we don't fight each other, not for any reason, ever. If you have a problem, or think something's unfair, you woof about it with me, and I'll resolve things.

"Rufus was wrong to take an extra kibble, so he'll lose one kibble at the next meal." Shep glared down at Rufus, who cowered and whimpered his agreement.

"As for the rest of the pack," Shep continued, "I know it's hard not getting all the kibble you're used to, but this storm has wrecked our world. We all miss our masters and mistresses, but the humans are gone. We dogs need to sacrifice so that we all can survive."

"Until when, Shep?" the little papillon, Rosie, yipped. "How long are we going to stay here?"

"Until our families come back," he woofed, "which will be soon, I hope. But until that sun, we dogs are all we have. We have to rely on each other, each dog standing nose-to-nose with his packmates. This den is our home, and we are each other's family."

For a heartbeat, the dogs wavered. Then they began to wag their tails and the smell of fear receded. They all looked at him with a strange awe, especially the new pack members, ones who hadn't seen him fight the wild dogs. Shep opened his jowls and panted lightly to let every dog know that he wasn't angry, and that everything was fine. And everything *was* fine. The crowd began to break up.

Paulie loped over to Shep's side from where he'd been standing near the entry to the main den, panting lightly, a knowing grin on his jowls. "I sensed you were a fellow fight dog," he woofed. "Glad to know there's an alpha with real power leading this pack."

The dog nodded his snout then got back into line. Shep felt a warmth spread from his chest out through his whole body. He'd solved a problem on his own, saved the pack without Callie's help. A smile twisted his jowls.

Callie burst from between the legs of some larger dogs and scrambled to Shep's side. "Great piles of biscuits, that was a mess!" she barked. "But you were marvelous!" She looked at Rufus, who still cringed against the wall. "I expected better from you, Rufus," she growled. "How can we get the new rescues to trust us if the original pack can't follow the rules?"

"I'm sorry!" Rufus cried. "Take all my kibble! Just stop growling at me!"

Callie sighed. "Oh, stop it, you old tail dragger." She nipped his neck. "Don't say things you don't mean — unless you *want* us to take all your kibble?"

Rufus rolled to his paws, still cowering low to the metal floor. "No," he squealed. "I don't want that."

"Fine," Callie woofed, "then go back to your den and think about all the trouble you caused by being greedy."

Shep wondered why Callie was barking about all this. He had solved the problem without her. Did she need to stick her snout into everything? *That's not thinking like a team*, Shep growled to himself. He shouldn't let one success make him think he's the Great Wolf.

Callie checked in with Higgins, who was completely frazzled.

"We need to assign a dog to sit here with me," he moaned. "Some big and mean-looking chap!"

"What we need is to set up some system so the whole pack isn't fighting for their kib every meal," woofed Callie.

"My thoughts exactly," added Shep.

Callie looked at him as if she'd forgotten he was there. "Right," she yipped. "Maybe we three should meet to try to dig up any other problems we might face before they bite us in the tail."

Shep and Higgins woofed their agreement.

"Let's sniff each other out after every dog's had their kibble," Callie barked. "Meet in the ceiling room, at the top of the table-ramp."

As Shep licked the last morsels of his kibble from his jowls, Oscar bounded up to him with a gangly boxer puppy at his heels.

"What's nibbling at you, pup?" Shep woofed.

"This is Odie," Oscar yipped. "And he and I just had this great idea." Oscar was wriggling and twitching like a squirrel's tail. He looked at Odie, then stood tall (as tall as he could on his stumpy legs). "We were thinking of starting a club!" He leapt up and started wagging his tail and yipping. Odie jumped on him and they rolled and played.

"A club?" Shep woofed, watching the two scrabble at his paws. "What kind of club?"

"A club about you!" Odie woofed in a scratchy, but surprisingly deep bark. "We were all just so washed away by how you handled that kibble fight, and then Oscar started telling us about how you fought a whole pack of wild dogs —"

"I didn't fight a whole pack," Shep interrupted.

"Yes," Oscar yowled, "he did fight a whole pack! We were all there, and we were throwing stuff at the dogs, but Shep was the only one in the mix, tearing the fur off those stinky wild dogs!"

"That's just the best-furred thing I've ever heard!" yelped Odie, his stump tail wagging.

Odie was older than Oscar, and much bigger. Shep sensed that Oscar was trying to fit in with the bigger pup by telling stories, nosing his way up the ranks by riding on the alpha's tail. But Shep felt bad about not sharing his den with the pup, and the little scrapper was always hanging on Shep's every woof. *It'd be good for him to make some other friends*, Shep thought.

"Well, all right," Shep woofed quietly. "Oscar here *is* telling the truth." He panted gently and licked Oscar's head. *That'll show Odie how well-furred Oscar is.* "I fought a whole pack of wild dogs, and bested their alpha in a fight, dog against dog."

"Holy treats!" Odie yipped. "Tell me everything!"

Shep woofed the whole story, with Oscar interjecting his own yips. Shep even allowed the pup to embellish things — how many dogs Shep fought, the size of Kaz's teeth, whether he'd beaten Zeus before the wave struck. What harm could it do to help the pup impress his new packmate?

Shep loped to the main den, padded up the table-ramp, and discovered Callie woofing softly with Higgins.

"Shep!" she barked, sounding surprised to see him. "Higgins and I were just going over the food stores."

Shep felt like he'd started playing with some dogs who'd rather he'd stayed by the fence. "What's wrong with the kibble stores?"

"Nothing," yapped Higgins. "I just wanted to woof numbers with Callie, you know, how many dogs and how much kibble per sun."

"Why didn't you wait for me?" Shep woofed. "I know about numbers."

"No doubt," Higgins snuffled, though the tone of his bark oozed doubt.

There was an awkward pause.

Callie stood, ears and tail low. "You're right." She stepped toward him, tail wagging. "I should have waited for you."

She lay down at Shep's paws, rolling to expose her belly. "I'm sorry."

Shep wagged his tail and licked Callie's head. "No worries," he woofed, feeling better after her show of submission. "What's the problem?"

Higgins yapped on about how they weren't scavenging enough kibble to feed every member of the pack sufficiently. "Much of the human kibble has gone to rot, and what's left will soon be inedible. We have to find another food source."

Callie's curled tail wagged in wide circles. "We can hunt!" she barked. "I could show some of the smaller dogs how I caught that squirrel, and maybe Dover could teach the big dogs. He said he's hunted with his master."

Shep's stomach soured at the thought. He dreaded eating lifeblood for every meal. *What if it turns me?* He'd managed to avoid going wild in the kibble den, but Shep worried that so much lifeblood pulsing through his body every sun might be enough to push him over to the nightmare of the Black Dog.

"I don't think that's a good idea," Shep woofed. "Lifeblood for every meal? It could turn the dogs wild, and they're already tearing into each other's scruffs for kibble."

Higgins coughed. "This pack would never go wild," he snapped. "We're civilized dogs." He jutted out his furface.

"We'll see how civilized things are when the kibble runs out," Shep grunted.

"Exactly," Callie woofed. "This is why we need to start hunting now. We can keep back some of the human kibble to mix in with the hunted meat and keep every dog's fur about them."

Shep licked his jowls. Higgins was right; with each passing sun, they found less and less kibble, and the pack continued to grow. They needed more food, and the only food out there was scurrying around on four legs.

"All right," Shep woofed. "We'll have to train some hunting dogs. Maybe Blaze can help. She's spent her whole life chasing after beasts."

"Double brilliant!" Callie yapped, getting excited about the whole hunting project, enough so that she seemed to forget how much she detested Blaze.

Callie began listing all the things they could hunt. "We'll have to have small, fast dogs for taking down squirrels and other rodents. Maybe the big dogs could catch a giant iguana — one of those could feed half the pack! And Shep, you could eat bugs! I found one earlier in my den. They're delicious and don't have any lifeblood."

"No thanks," Shep said, remembering the long, shiny black things he'd sometimes seen in his boy's den. "I'll manage on the squirrel meat."

Callie's tail drooped. "I'm telling you, the bugs are really tasty."

Shep panted and licked her snout. "You've got interesting tastes," he yipped. "Lizards, bugs. Next you'll be telling me how delicious trees are."

Callie cocked her head. "I hadn't even thought of trees. Brilliant, Shep!"

Shep's tail slumped. *Great Wolf, strike me down with your paw before I eat a tree.*

As the moon passed over the windowed ceiling of the room, the three dogs argued and chattered. It was determined that the dogs needed to be divided into teams. One team would train with Callie, Blaze, and Dover in hunting. Another team, led by Virgil, would maintain defenses. A third team would keep up with the scavenging and rescue operation, headed by Honey. Shep would work with Virgil and also keep every dog in line with the plan. At mealtimes, the dogs would eat with their teams, and each team would rotate being the first in line for kibble.

By the time the three had finished planning, it was the middle of the night.

"We shouldn't wake every dog," Callie woofed, exhausted. "Shep, you make the announcements in the morning."

He agreed, his woof broken mid-bark by a yawn. "I need some sleep," he groaned.

"I'm already half-zonked," grunted Higgins. He crept down the table-ramp toward his den.

Shep began to follow, then saw Callie heading in the other direction. "You coming to bed?" he woofed.

"I just want to check with Boji on how those dams are doing."

Shep waved his tail. "Smell you in the sunlight," he snuffled.

Callie wagged her tail back. "Good night, partner."

When Shep returned to his den, he found Blaze already curled in a corner.

"Where've you been?" she woofed. "I waited for you after getting my kibble."

"I had a meeting about the pack," Shep replied, curling next to her. Dim moonlight from the small ceiling window shone in her eyes.

"A meeting?" Blaze shuffled around so her snout was near Shep's. "With whom? About what?"

"Just pack stuff," Shep grunted. "Callie, Higgins, and I worked everything out."

"Higgins?" Blaze lifted her head. "Why didn't you invite me to come if Higgins was there?"

Shep smelled the anger wafting off Blaze. "Higgins was there to woof about the food stores," he said softly, trying to calm her. "It wasn't a big meeting. I wasn't trying to nose you out."

Blaze laid her head back on her paws. "Fine," she woofed. "But I don't smell why you need to meet with them at all." She licked her jowls. "Callie wasn't the one who broke up that fight. You did, and all on your own." Her breath ruffled the tiny hairs in his ear. "This pack would throw themselves into the canal if you barked for them to. Not for Callie or Higgins — just for you."

Shep wondered if that was true. Recalling the look in

Paulie's eyes after the kibble fight, he thought Blaze might be right. If even a tough dog like Paulie looked ready to throw himself to a water lizard on Shep's command, what horrors would a weakling like Rufus or Snoop be willing to suffer for him? Anxiety flooded Shep's mind. He tried to remember what he'd woofed earlier — he was never careful enough with his barks. What if he'd said the wrong thing? The power he'd felt running through him suddenly felt terrible and cold, heavy like a coat of metal.

"That's not how things are, Blaze," Shep woofed, giving back whatever role she was trying to collar him with. "Every dog has a say in the way the pack's run."

"You're the alpha, Shep." Blaze looked straight into his muzzle. "Never forget it."

She sat up and stared out the window in the ceiling, up at the Silver Moon. "On the beast farm, there were strict rules about who could give commands. Each man to his dog, and one man to all the other men. One sun, two men had a disagreement. They gave conflicting signals to their dogs, and the stupid mutts drove two groups of stray cattle into one another. The herd stampeded, and the two dogs and one of the men were trampled. The man was healed. I never saw either of the dogs again."

Blaze looked away, at the dark corner opposite Shep. "I lost a good friend that sun."

Shep wasn't sure why she was telling him about this. "Was he your mate?" he asked, waving his tail in what he hoped was a sensitive and caring way.

"That's not the point," Blaze snapped, turning her muzzle to face Shep. A deep sadness was visible in her shining eyes. "Dogs are not meant to follow two masters. They need an alpha to guide them. Without that, we're all as good as trampled."

She looked fiercely into Shep's muzzle, waiting for his reply.

"Callie and I are a good team," Shep woofed, finally. "We've protected the pack for this many suns. We'll all be okay."

Blaze's jaw was set, like she was about to argue, but then she flopped onto her chest and curled in her paws. "I only hope you're right," she snuffled.

CHAPTER 9
DEFENSIVE MOVES

The dogs assigned to the defense team rambled out of the boat and sat in the plaza. Shep watched them from the shade of a collapsed wall held up by a leafless palm tree. There were ten dogs assigned to the team, all chosen by Shep. They were the toughest of the pack, by the smell of them — some big, like Hulk, some small, like Daisy — but Shep had no idea if any of them knew the first thing about defending a den. He wasn't quite sure himself what the job entailed.

Daisy strutted her way across the stone, lifting her paw pads high off the already steamy pavement. "So what's — *snort* — the plan?" she yapped, collapsing into a sit with one hind leg splayed.

What is the plan, indeed, thought Shep.

Two big dogs — a stout black short-haired dog with red-brown markings Shep had only smelled the other sun and a sleek black and brown Doberman girldog Virgil liked, named Ripley — began to play with one another in the shade of the boat. Shep watched one bat at the other's head, then tumble on the ground and start up play again. He thought of what he would do if he'd been playing with those dogs, how he would've reared for a better angle of attack, how a glancing swipe at a muzzle isn't worth a ripped toy if it isn't a feint toward a better hold on the scruff.

It was like Shep had uncovered a buried bag of kibble. These were just the kinds of tips these dogs needed to know. They all knew how to play, but now they needed to know how to turn play into defense.

"Dogs!" he barked, standing tall. "Come over here by this tree."

Shep divided the dogs into pairs, matching each with a dog of similar size. The dogs loped into their assigned groups, then looked at Shep with vacant expressions or stared off over the canal. A strange bird with loud, whirly wings chopped through the air high overhead. It was the loudest thing Shep had heard since the storm, and he had to raise his bark over the sound until it flew away.

"We need to think of defense as play, but play with a bite," Shep woofed.

"I haven't smelled anything bigger than a rat in suns," the black short-hair barked. "What do we need to defend this den from?"

Some of the others snorted and wagged their tails in agreement.

Another Rufus, Shep grumbled to himself. *This pack needs another tail dragger like it needs a flea infestation.*

"What's your name?" Shep asked.

The black dog stood tall, feeling a little more sure of himself now that Shep was barking directly to him. "Panzer," he woofed. "Anyway, I'm a rottweiler. What's going to mess with me?"

"Well, Panzer, have you ever fought a rat?" Shep snapped. "What if one came into our den to scavenge our food? What would you do?"

Panzer sneered at Shep's domineering tone. "I'd tear the thing's tail off. I'm a trained guard dog." He looked at Shep with a smug smirk on his jowls.

So this dog has some skills — I'll let him think he's got something over me. "Oh," woofed Shep, feigning awe. "Would you be so kind as to show me?"

Panzer strutted forward, nose in the air and tail flat. Shep sank into a slight crouch. When Panzer was a stretch away, Shep lunged forward, hitting Panzer with his forepaws and knocking him onto his side.

"Hey!" yipped Panzer. "I wasn't ready!"

"No dog or rat or flea who's invading our den cares if you're ready," Shep growled, standing over the toppled Panzer. "A fight — I mean, a defense dog is ready every heartbeat of every sun."

Panzer got to his paws and shook his fur. "That was a cheap bite," he snarled. "If you're just going to nose us around, I'm heading back into the den."

Daisy gave Shep a concerned head tilt.

Shep lowered his stance and wagged his tail. "You're right," he woofed. "I'm sorry, Panzer."

Daisy wagged her knot of a tail. "Let's — *snort* — get this play-biting started!"

Panzer licked his jowls, as if thinking about whether to challenge Shep any further. "Apology accepted," he grunted, finally.

Shep decided that maybe he would do better with some in-the-heartbeat instruction, as opposed to leading a general lesson. He told the pairs of dogs to play with each other.

"Just go with it," he woofed.

Paulie the pitbull dove for Hulk's scruff, latching on with a fierce grip of the jaws.

"Shep!" Hulk whimpered. "It hurts!"

Shep pounced on Paulie, knocking his hold.

"What?" Paulie whined, licking and smacking his jaws. "You said fight."

"*Play* fight," Shep woofed, panting with exasperation. "I know you're an ex-fight dog, but don't actually tear any dog's ear off! For the love of treats, we're all in the same pack."

The dogs began playing, some more timidly than others, a mere paw slap here and there. Shep began to wonder if this training plan was going to work after all.

Shep trotted up to Bernie and a midsized girldog, who were just sitting looking at one another. "What's wrong?" he woofed. "Why aren't you playing?"

"The border collie keeps nipping at my paws," Bernie grumbled. "I don't like any dog touching my paws."

"My name's Jazz," the girldog snapped. "And that's how I play, dainty-paw."

"Call me that again, fur-for-brains," Bernie growled.

Shep stuck his snout between them. "Whoa," he woofed. "Let's just back away."

Bernie and Jazz stepped back, lowering hackles and tails, and taking less hostile stances.

"Let's smell if we can't use this," Shep woofed. "If rats were attacking, they'd probably go for your paws. What would be the best defense?" He lowered his snout to the stone and looked up at Bernie. "Come on," Shep yipped. "Take a swipe at my snout."

Bernie, confused, took a feeble swipe at Shep's snout with his paw. Shep snapped at Bernie's claws, careful not to land a tooth on his pads.

"Hey!" Bernie cried, jerking his paw away.

"I wasn't going to bite you," Shep woofed, "but that defense was terrible. You protected one paw by opening the other to attack. It would have been better to have come down with your fangs and attacked my head from above, away from my jaws. I couldn't have defended myself from that without backing away from your paw and changing my head angle."

Bernie raised his ears and tilted his head, impressed. "And if you were a rat, I could have grabbed you and tossed you away."

"Exactly!" Shep barked. "That's the kind of thinking we have to start doing. Team!" Shep howled. "Let's all practice this move Jazz and Bernie worked out."

The teams practiced over and over the paw defense, as the dogs called it, and by midsun, all were expert rat catchers. Virgil and Ripley even came up with the double-trouble paw defense, an attack from above with fangs, and from the side with hind claws. Shep felt like he was finally on the right scent with training the team.

The pavement was getting unbearably hot, so Shep brought the team into the shade of the crushed floor where at least the sun wasn't burning their fur. They woofed about the practical aspects of defense — setting up watches, how to protect the two entrances — then Shep had the teams nose some of the more dangerous scraps of wreckage away from the door holes. As Shep was helping to dig a pile of sticks out from under a plastic cushion, Oscar came wriggling out from the main den.

"Watch it, pup!" Shep woofed. "We're moving sharp stuff. I don't want to have to send Boji another injured paw to lick."

Oscar dropped his snout and sniffed at the floor, eyes scouring the surface in front of his paws, so that he walked right into Shep's hind leg.

"Sorry!" he yipped. "But I was careful, just like you said!"

Shep panted lightly. "Careful of one danger, but you

walked right into another. What if I'd been an enemy intruder?"

"But you'll never let an enemy get into the den, Shep," Oscar woofed, tail swinging. "You're my Great Wolf! Defender of the weak dog! Protector of the pups!" He leapt in little circles, yipping and growling and tackling imaginary foes.

Shep grinned at the pup's display. "All right," he woofed. "What's got you scampering out of the den?"

"Some of the other pups saw the defense team fighting. I was wondering if we could all come out and watch?"

Shep glanced around the crushed floor. They were almost done clearing the entries and arranging the rubble. "Sure," he barked. "I'll take the team out and work on some real fight skills."

"Ha-roo!" Oscar howled. "I have to tell every pup!" He scrambled back into the main den. Just as he was about to disappear through the hole, he looked over his tail. "Did you see, Shep?" he yipped. "I was looking at my paws *and* in front of me that time!"

Shep barked that he'd done a great job, then bayed for the defense team to move out to the street again. The sun was low, as it was nearly sunset, and the surrounding buildings shaded the plaza.

They divided into pairs again and Shep began barking about how to defend against a dog attack.

"The key is to keep your stance loose," Shep woofed, bouncing lightly on his paws. He glanced at the small pack of pups huddled in the shadows near the crushed floor and gave Oscar a quick flick of the muzzle. The pup nearly knocked himself over, his tail was wagging so hard.

Shep continued, "And to use any attack to your advantage by mastering the roll." He fell onto his side, rolled, and sprang back onto his paws.

Several of the defense dogs tilted their heads in confusion. Shep rolled again, slower.

"Do you tuck your paws before or after you hit the street?" whined Ripley.

"Just roll, like this," Paulie barked.

He rolled masterfully, as did Panzer — but they were both trained fight dogs. A fight dog couldn't survive without knowing how to roll. The others simply flopped onto their sides, then scrambled to get back onto their paws. There was no rolling involved.

"No!" barked Shep. "Don't push against the street with your paws, Mooch. Throw them over your belly." Mooch was gigantic, and when she fell over, Shep felt the vibration in his paws.

The team looked like a bunch of beetles flipped onto their shells. Paulie tried to explain how to roll, but he didn't have the patience for every dog's clumsiness. His instruction degraded into a series of nasty barks.

Shep heard the pups panting and saw them tumbling over one another like Balls in a basket. *What am I doing wrong that I can't get these big dogs to do what they naturally did as pups?*

The defense team just could not get the concept of the roll. Shep tried demonstrating the move in slow-motion again and explaining how he used his muscles: Nothing worked. Waffle, the brown and white spotted mutt, could roll like a Ball when lying down, but fell like a stone when he tried to do it starting on all fours. Most of the team, though, couldn't have rolled in any position for all the cheese in a cold box.

In his frustration, Shep thought of Zeus, of how he'd known all of these moves without thinking, as instinctive to him as panting. Shep imagined training these dogs with Zeus. Zeus would have known just what to bark to get a pant out of the pack. Zeus would have made this fun.

Of course, Shep reminded himself, *that was the old Zeus.* That dog had become the wild Zeus, the dog who tried to kill him.

As the sky turned from orange to deep blue, Shep called off the practice. He could smell that the team was in a foul mood — no dog liked feeling like a failure.

"Great work, team," he woofed, a happy grin on his jowls and a light wag in his tail. No dog responded; not a single tail wagged back.

Mooch and Panzer offered to take first watch. Shep told Virgil to dismiss the rest of the team.

"Excellent work," Virgil woofed, as he loped back into the main den at Shep's flank.

"What do you mean?" groaned Shep. "Every dog was ready to scratch my fur off after that terrible practice."

"Let them whine," woofed Virgil. "They'll be thanking

you when they can roll away from an attack. You came up with a good method. That's why you're the alpha." Virgil trotted off, sniffing around the main den, barking at any dog who was taking up too much space.

The alpha. The words slipped off Shep's coat like raindrops. His idea had worked because he hadn't tried to be the alpha; he'd let the whole team work on the defense tactics together. But then, Shep wondered, could that also be a way of leading the dogs? Was sharing power one way of being an alpha? Blaze would have barked absolutely not, that this was exactly the kind of thinking that got her friends killed. But that was a human-dog, maybe a human-dog-beast, problem. Maybe when it was just dogs, it was better to work as a team. It certainly smelled better than trying to bark orders to every dog.

Honey trotted straight up to Shep with Fuzz perched, as usual, on her back.

"We had such a great sun!" she woofed. "Five new rescues! I'm sorry to report that we haven't had much luck getting any other species to join us, so it's just dogs, but Fuzz and I will keep trying! Fuzz nearly convinced this very poofy white cat named Ares, but he hissed something so rude that Fuzz wouldn't even translate it for me. I almost got a pet hamster to come with us, but she seemed to misunderstand Fuzz's greeting and ran into a hole in the wall."

Honey waved her tail, waiting for Shep to praise her efforts. Shep wasn't sure exactly what to bark. He didn't want to go back on his word to her, but he was also immensely grateful that no other cats or — Great Wolf forbid — hamsters accepted her offer of protection.

"Great job," he woofed, finally. "I'm sure you'll have better luck next sun."

"Me, too!" Honey barked. "Fuzz and I are going to spend all night working on our pitch."

Fuzz didn't say anything, but as Honey turned, he stared at Shep with his strange, green cat-eyes, boring into Shep's fur like a tick. Shep had a feeling Fuzz knew that he had no interest in any more cats or rats joining the pack. Shep just hoped Fuzz had the decency not to share this insight with Honey.

Honey was a perfect example of how forcing an idea down every dog's throat came back to bite you in the tail. Shep should have let every dog vote on Fuzz joining the pack. Then the decision wouldn't rest entirely on Shep's back. *Note to self,* Shep mused, *if every dog votes for it, no dog can blame the alpha!*

CHAPTER 10
GROWL OF THE STORM SHAKER

With each sun's practice, the defense team improved. On the third sun, Shep divided the group into two teams and had them take turns either defending the den's two entrances or attacking them.

Shep watched the exercises from the shade of an overhang. "That's it, Waffle!" he cried. "Roll, then kick with your hind legs." Waffle had Ripley in a good scruff hold, and managed to keep her from sneaking up on him over the steering counter.

Snoop stuck his skinny head out of the stairwell hole and nearly got his nose bitten off by Panzer.

"Agh! Shep!" he yelped, dodging Panzer's fangs. "Higgins-sent-me-to-get-you-there's-trouble-with-the-kibble-and —"

"Shut your snout!" Shep howled. He scrambled over to

Snoop. "Never woof that there's a kibble problem," he snuffled. "Do you want to cause a frenzy?"

Snoop cowered. "Sorry-Shep-I-just-woofed-what-Higgins-said-to-bark."

Shep sighed. Snoop wasn't exactly the sharpest tooth in the jaw, though he always meant well. "Just tell me what the problem is," Shep woofed.

Snoop explained that Higgins had noticed a few missing kibbles from the pile. When he investigated further, he found that the window in the floor had cracked under the weight of the food. Some bites had fallen under the boat and attracted rats.

"He-thought-maybe-the-defense-team-could-get-the-rats?" Snoop yipped. "The-hunters-are-all-out-hunting."

"I couldn't have planned a better first test for the team," Shep barked.

Shep called the defense dogs together. Virgil and Ripley were left to guard the crushed floor, while the rest all shuffled down the stairwell to the kibble room.

Higgins was practically frothing with worry when the team arrived. "What took you so long?" he snapped. "The nasty squeakers have been trying to creep out of their hole, but I've whapped them back, the scoundrels!"

Higgins and Snoop had rolled the food away from the window. The hole in the window was much too small for the majority of the team to get more than a paw or snout through. Even Daisy would have trouble jamming her fat neck through the hole.

"We're all too big," Shep grumbled. "I think we have to wait for the hunting teams to return. Maybe Callie and some of her small hunters could fit down there."

"Shep-dog no wait," hissed Fuzz, who padded into the room. "Fuzz have idea."

Shep sneered at the cat. *Where'd he come from?* "Why aren't you out with Honey?" he asked.

"Ate bad bug last night," Fuzz meowed. "Fuzz stomach like Shep-dog's brain — full of knots." He hissed a high-pitched cackle.

"Your idea?" Shep growled.

Fuzz shot Shep a snarky look, like Shep should have laughed at Fuzz's insult. Then he hiss-barked his plan. "Dog-with-fur-for-nose have things all wrong," he meow-barked. "Fuzz go down hole, then scare rats up to big snarl-and-drool dogs, yes? Then dog eat rat."

Daisy sniffed the edge of the hole. "Could — *snort* — work," she yapped. "Not like any dog has a better idea."

Before any other dog could so much as grunt a response, Fuzz was through the broken window and down into the dark. There was some hissing, some squeaking, a loud meow, and then the first rat burst out from the window hole and scurried for the pile of food.

The stupid squeaker never knew what bit him, Jazz was on him so fast. With a snap of her jaw, the rat fell still. Jazz dropped it onto the kibble pile.

"One down, countless more kibbles to go!" she barked with excitement.

There was more meowing and hissing and squeaking, and soon the rats were popping out of the window hole like kibbles from a bag. The defense team tore into them, shredding each rat into bites for the food pile. Shep chased one intrepid rodent into the hall and massacred it against the wall, leaving a splatter of lifeblood.

As they ravaged the rats, a feeling welled up inside Shep. Not the blind fury of the fight cage, but a satisfaction, like the whole world was his for the sniffing. And it was different from the glow he felt after giving a speech and having all the dogs stare up at him. That glow also weighed him down like a golden collar — he shouldered so much responsibility when he led the pack. The rush he felt hunting down the squeakers was pure energy — light and fiery. Was this what Frizzle had felt all those suns ago? Shep felt like the whole world was full of good things, and that they were all for him. Attacking this measly rat, surrounded by strong dogs who listened to his barks — he *was* the Great Wolf.

The pack was glad for the extra rat-kibble that night, and Shep actually looked forward to the nightly meeting of the team leaders. *Maybe tonight we won't have to listen to Higgins whine about food rations.*

Shep crossed the main den and overheard Ginny woofing to some other small dogs about Lassie. He heard his name mentioned, and the Great Wolf, and decided to eavesdrop on the group — he had a few heartbeats until the meeting started. He lay down behind an overturned couch so he could listen undetected.

Ginny's squeaky bark pierced the darkness. "As Oscar has told us, when dogs most need guidance, the Silver Moon sends us a leader. First there was the Great Wolf, who saved dogs from turning wild, then came Lassie, who helped dogs and humans live together, and now, in our time of need, she has sent us Shep, the Storm Shaker."

And then she launched into a story that sounded all too familiar to Shep.

There came a time when the sky chased the humans from their dens. Their fear of the angry sky drove them to leave quickly, and in their hurry, they were unable to bring more than they could carry on their bodies: They had to leave all their dogs behind.

Dogs had not lived on their own in many cycles. The Great Wolf saw their distress, and the fierce sky that threatened them, and knew something needed to be done. He curled himself tighter around the Silver Moon, and shook free some moonstuff. Then he searched for a dog who might be worthy of such a gift.

The Great Wolf saw the Storm Shaker on the street and watched. The Storm Shaker did not fear the winds and rain —he walked boldly through them. He cared for his fellow dogs — he traveled with a small companion. The Great Wolf decided to test the Storm Shaker's muster. He fashioned the moonstuff into a vicious bird of prey and sent it to attack the companion. The Storm Shaker descended upon the bird in a fury of teeth and claws. The bird was easily vanquished and the companion saved. The Great Wolf knew then that he had found a worthy dog. He licked the hide of the Storm Shaker, and with that lick, gave him the magic moonstuff.

The Storm Shaker felt its power swell within him. Soon, no door or boundary could keep him from his task of saving trapped dogs. The sky raged, tearing buildings to pieces; the Storm Shaker raged, tearing doors from their hinges to free his packmates.

The fierce winds blew through the darkest caves under the city, and so strong did they blow that they reached the lair of the Black Dog. The winds carried the scent of the Great Wolf's moonstuff on the Storm Shaker's hide.

So the Great Wolf has chosen a champion, *the Black Dog thought*. I must smell this new hero. *He slunk from the blackest shadows and crept after the scent.*

The Storm Shaker's scent led him to a building. The Black Dog wanted to scare the Storm Shaker, so he turned into a shrieking wind and attacked the building, tearing apart its walls. But the Storm Shaker was not afraid. He looked the fierce wind in the muzzle and snarled back at its whirling fangs.

The Black Dog was impressed by the Storm Shaker. He ruminated upon a new means to destroy the Great Wolf's Champion. He scratched his black hide and stiff hairs fell onto the street. The Black Dog blew upon the hairs and they each grew into a snarling, snapping wild dog.

"Are you hungry, my children?" the Black Dog asked. And

the newly grown dogs, grotesque and growling, howled their assent.

"Then you must find the Storm Shaker," the Black Dog replied. "The Storm Shaker has stolen your kibble."

The wild pack tore after the Storm Shaker's scent. They found him in a cavernous den and attacked him with all their strength and ferocity. The Storm Shaker and his packmates fought bravely against the wild dogs. The Black Dog looked on, surprised by the Storm Shaker's defense, and knew something more needed to be done. He licked the fur of one of his wild dogs, and that dog swelled to twice the size of a normal dog.

The monstrous girldog's fangs glistened. "What is your bidding, master?" she snarled.

"You must defeat the Storm Shaker," the Black Dog answered.

"It is done," she growled.

The girldog, a full head taller than the rest of the wild pack, loped through their ranks, and the wild dogs stepped aside, letting her pass. The Storm Shaker stood tall, his ears forward and brave muzzle high.

"I do not want to fight my fellow dog," the Storm Shaker barked, his voice clear and sonorous.

"Then I will kill you with a single bite," the girldog snarled.

"I do not want to fight," the Storm Shaker replied, "but I will always defend my pack, even if it means my very life."

The girldog lunged at the Storm Shaker with her sharp fangs. The Storm Shaker spread his strong jaws and bit into her shaggy *neck. With a jerk of his head, he took the life from the girldog. She withered like a popped Ball, then fell to the floor; she was again merely a hair.*

The Black Dog bellowed with anger. He saw that these phantom dogs were no match for the Storm Shaker. He needed a real dog, and what better dog than the Storm Shaker's best friend?

The Black Dog licked the hide of the friend, a proud dog named Zeus. The Black Dog coursed through Zeus's veins like poison, and he became like the Black Dog — ruthless and wild.

"I challenge you!" Zeus cried. "I challenge the Storm Shaker!"

The Storm Shaker bowed his great head. A heavy sadness came over him. He did not want to fight his friend. But then he saw the frightened eyes of his packmates and knew that he had to defend them, no matter the cost.

The Storm Shaker answered the Black Dog Zeus's challenge, and they fought a battle that shook the very earth their paws stood upon. Then the Storm Shaker reared, and crashed down on the Black Dog like a boulder, and Zeus fell still against the floor. The Black Dog's spirit slithered out of Zeus, a vile shadow across the stone, and into the night, finally defeated.

The Storm Shaker stood over his friend, and wept. His packmates joined him and their tears flowed. Their sadness was so great, the tears became as a flood and washed over the city like a wave.

The Great Wolf, moved by the dogs' mourning, took up Zeus's spirit to join him as a companion of the Silver Moon. The Storm Shaker thanked the Great Wolf and pledged to always protect any animal who needed help. In return, the Great Wolf dried the flood of tears so that the dogs might live again in the city.

"All praise the Silver Moon," moaned the other dogs. "All praise Shep."

Shep was numb with shock. Oscar had made him into the Great Wolf's Champion? What madness had taken hold of the pup?

The dogs rose and trotted off to their various beds. Shep emerged from the shadows just as Ginny was about to hop into her own nest of pillows.

"Shep!" she cried, flustered. "I hardly ever smell you at this end of the den."

"What was that I just heard you saying to those dogs?" His bark trembled.

"Do you like it?" she woofed, tail waving and eyes sparkling with excitement. "It's a story that Oscar and I have piled together. We thought that the dogs might like a story to help them in these dark times. 'Storm Shaker.' Isn't that deliciously dramatic? It was my contribution!"

"But it's crazy," Shep woofed. "I'm made of moonstuff from the Silver Moon?"

"It's not crazy," Ginny said, standing tall, defensive. "Why is it crazy to want to believe your leader is powerful, and powerful in a way that no other dog could be? It gives the old dogs and the pups a measure of comfort to think of you as an all-powerful defender of the pack."

Shep thought about this. He'd been comforted by the old timer's tales of the Great Wolf back in the fight kennel. Why deny the members of his own pack a similar comfort?

"You're right," he woofed, dropping his stance. "Just remember to tell them that it's only a story."

"Of course," Ginny yipped, standing again and waving her tail. "Every dog knows it's just a story."

On trembling paws, Shep sniffed out Callie in the room at the top of the table-ramp where the team leaders — Virgil, Higgins, and Honey (who was always accompanied by Fuzz) — met every night. Callie was the only one there. She sat staring up at the large window in the ceiling.

"I'm just finishing up telling Frizzle about my sun," Callie barked, dropping her muzzle to look at Shep. "I always think of him, romping around with the Great Wolf, sparkling in the sky, the way we imagined him." She looked out the window again. "Before the storm, there were always so many lights in the city, you could never see the lights in the sky. But now, it looks like the city is in the sky, and we're caught in the darkness."

Shep slapped his paw on the light switch and soft yellow lights began to glow. "Now it's light," he yipped, grinning, trying to hide how shaken he was by Ginny's woofs.

Callie panted lightly. "That's not what I mean, silly fur," she barked. "Turn the lights off. I want to see the moon-stuff glitter."

Shep slapped the switch again, then padded to Callie's side and looked up at the Great Wolf's shimmering coat.

"I overheard Ginny telling this crazy story," Shep woofed.

"I've heard it," Callie yipped. "I thought you'd like it, being barked into the Great Wolf's legend."

"No," Shep said quietly. "It's not right. The Great Wolf's legend is special. It means something to me." Shep looked down at the shadows. "Oscar should have asked me before making up such scat."

"It's just a story," Callie grunted.

But it wasn't just a story, Shep wanted to woof. He really believed that the Great Wolf watched over him. The look on Callie's muzzle, however, made clear that she had no idea what he was barking about. And he didn't know how to make her smell that sometimes a story became more than just a story, that sometimes the story became real.

Callie and Shep sat there for several heartbeats, lost in their private trails of thought, no sound but the paw-slaps and chatter of the pack in the den beyond.

Higgins shuffled up the table-ramp, full of bad-smelling news. He waited for Virgil and Honey (and Fuzz), who were close on his tail, then began his grumbling.

First, there was the problem of food shortages.

"But we caught all those rats," Shep moaned.

Higgins sniffed his furface. "It's not that there's not enough food for the pack," he woofed. "It's that the pack is constantly growing and most of the new dogs are half-starved, half-fur-brained with fear, or missing half their parts!"

"We're all survivors of this storm," snapped Honey, whose bark became a squeal as she became defensive. "Just because we find these dogs suns after the storm doesn't mean they're any less worthy of our help."

"Boji's losing patches of fur, she's so frantic trying to heal the new recruits," woofed Virgil.

"Maybe we need to reallocate the dogs," Callie yipped. "Maybe some of the older dogs who can't hunt can help Boji with wound licking? And then we can move some of the search and rescue dogs to hunting to help with getting more kibble."

"But we also search for food," whined Honey. "My team is the most important."

"You're bringing in less kibble every sun," Higgins grumbled. "And most of what you bring me is rotten beyond being edible."

"I can switch to hunting," woofed Shep, remembering that warm feeling during the rat massacre. "The defense team is training itself at this point."

"Good," barked Callie. "Honey, I'm taking Rosie, Reggie, and Speckles from your team."

Honey snorted, but Fuzz laid a paw on her tail and Honey quieted down.

Callie leaned her muzzle into Shep's ear. "I think you should woof something to the crowd," she snuffled, flicking her nose at the eyes glittering in the darkness along the table-ramp. Apparently, all their barking had attracted an audience. "Something reassuring," Callie added.

The strength rushed from Shep's legs. Hearing Ginny's story had thrown Shep like a toy. No matter what he woofed, he felt like the pack would take it the wrong way, like he was barking a message from the Great Wolf himself.

Callie raised her eyebrows, waiting for him to begin.

Shep exhaled, his jowls loose. "No dog needs to worry," he began loudly. "We're going to have more hunters. I promise, your bellies will be full by the next sunset!"

The pack yipped and howled with excitement and the crowd broke up, happy tails wagging.

"That wasn't exactly what I meant," growled Callie.

"You said reassure them," Shep snarled. "You don't like what I woof, come up with something more specific for me to bark. You've never had a problem doing that." He slunk down the table-ramp away from her.

Shep needed a scent of fresh air. The den suddenly felt small and stuffy. He wound his way through the dogs, ignoring the strange, awestruck looks on some of their muzzles as he passed, and bounded into the darkness. Near a small overturned boat by the water, he found Dover. Shep wagged his tail to ask if it'd be okay if he joined him, and Dover waved his tail that Shep could sit.

After many heartbeats, Shep interrupted the silence. "You sleep out here?" he woofed.

"It's quieter," the old timer replied.

Shep lay down and rested his snout on his paws. "Have you heard the stories?"

"About you?" Dover woofed, still looking out at the stars over the water.

Shep waved his tail.

"Yep," Dover said, lying down beside Shep. "I've heard."

"Should I stop Oscar and Ginny?"

"Not my Ball to catch," Dover woofed. "You'll know what to do when the time's right."

They lay beside each other under the glittering coat of the night sky. Every few heartbeats, a yapper-sized bat blacked out the Great Wolf's fires as it streaked through the dark. All around, crickets chirruped. A cat's screech echoed from an alley. The chopping *whump-whump* sound of one of the whirly birds echoed off the pavement.

CHAPTER 11
HUNTER AND HUNTED

Shep woke at first light. Dover yawned beside him, then waved his tail to say good morning. Shep looked across the plaza and saw that Blaze was already Outside. She sat by one of the water-filled boats, watching him. She flicked her tail.

"I missed you last night," she barked.

Shep rose, stretched, and loped to her side. "I've been assigned to your team," he woofed, "so you'll get to smell me all sun."

"Finally ready to try your fangs at a real job?" she asked.

"Real job?" Shep said, and lapped up a mouthful of rainwater. "What's so 'real' about your job? You're catching birds, squirrels. I've seen Cars catch them."

Blaze nipped his scruff. "Think you're such a well-furred

hunter, hero?" she snuffled in his ear. "I can't wait to smell this."

Shep nodded to the defense dogs on duty — Hulk and Paulie — as he trotted with Blaze out to where the hunting teams gathered. Callie sat woofing with Dover, and Blaze joined them. Shep followed.

"What do you think you're doing?" yipped Callie.

"Just sniffing what's happening." Shep was confused — wasn't he the alpha here?

"Get back with the trainees, Trainee Shepherd," barked Blaze. "We have to fit you into one of the beginner teams."

"Trainee?" Shep grumbled. "Beginner? I can catch more prey than any of these dogs."

"Really?" woofed Dover. "Then don't let us stand in your way." He waved his snout toward the street. "Smell you at midsun."

Shep loped away from the three, tail low. *They think I need training*, Shep grumbled as he walked down the Sidewalk. *I'm a born hunter. I'll show them.*

The farther he got from the other dogs, the better he felt. It was good to be Outside, alone, where there were no other dogs to bark orders to, or to worry about, or to listen to tell fur-brained stories.

He opened his nose and fully scented the air. Things were breathing in all the shadows around him — warm, living things. Leaves rustled in a bush, giving away the hiding place of an iguana. Birds cooed in the shadows under the eaves of a toppled roof.

All mine, thought Shep.

He decided to go for the warm things on the ground. Shep focused his nose. His options were a chipmunk in the scrub between two buildings, a clutch of mice hidden under chunks of a broken wall, and a squirrel chattering in a tree off toward sunrise. Shep decided to go for the chipmunk.

He stretched his lean muscles. With a spring like a Car from a streetlight, Shep dove into the bush. The chipmunk, however, scurried out from his scrape in the dirt. Shep's forelegs got tangled in the mesh of thin branches. He pulled himself out and darted after the rodent. It skittered under any object it could find, but Shep had its scent. He followed it down an alley. He had the thing cornered. *It's all over, my furry friend.*

The chipmunk shoved its way under a pile of rubble near the fence in the middle of the alley. Shep flopped onto the pavement and dug frantically. The scent of chipmunk was everywhere. Every heartbeat drove the lifeblood faster through Shep's body. His claws raked the stone and a splinter bit his paw pad. Still, he fought to snag the chipmunk's fur.

Then the scent was farther away. Shep struggled out and up, only to see the chipmunk, a blur of red-brown, running full speed down the alley on the opposite side of the fence.

Frustrated, Shep swiped at the pile of rubble, toppling part of it, and found himself nose to snout with one of the scaly floor-sucker tube creatures. It snapped its dark brown tube-body into a tight coil, raised its tail, and opened its wide, white mouth. Shep was unsure whether to run or bite. He growled at the tube and it shook its tail, creating an awful stench. Shep choked and stumbled back. The tube lowered its tail and uncurled slightly.

Giving up so easily, my scaly kibble? Shep thought, and prepared for a second assault.

"Step back," growled Blaze from behind him. "Use small steps until you're a stretch away, then run."

"From a tube?" Shep needed one, maybe two bites at most, to sever its neck.

"That thing's a snake," snuffled Blaze, "and it's a killer. One bite and a dog's done."

Her bark trembled and her ears were flat against her head. Shep had never smelled her so scared. He stepped away slowly, then ran. Blaze dashed behind him, close on his tail.

"A snake killed one of my herding partners," she woofed as they slowed to a trot. She looked at him with her sparkling eyes; in the sunlight, they seemed flecked with gold.

"I can take one measly snake bite," Shep said, grinning. He wanted to make her smile.

Blaze licked his nose. "Let's start you out hunting something a little less dead-making than a snake, okay, hero?" She loped ahead. "At least until you're not outwitted by a chipmunk."

"Outwitted?" Shep barked. "No way. The thing cheated! It ran under the trash pile!"

Blaze tipped her head slightly. "That's cheating?" she yipped. "If that's how you want to smell it, I won't tell any dog different." She smiled, then flicked her tail and ran down an alley.

They stopped in the street near one of the hunting teams. The leaders had organized the dogs on each team into different jobs. The lead dog was the best scent-spotter and identified all the possible prey, indicating the animals' hiding spots with a flick of the snout or tail. The remaining dogs broke off into pairs: one dog to scare the prey from its hiding place, the other to catch it as it tried to escape the first. At the rear of the group was the general tracker. If the prey escaped any of the pairs, that dog gave the prey chase until the pair could catch up and finish the job. It was a good system. Certainly better than Shep's method of singular failure. He spotted a bird, bounded after it, and ended up getting a mouthful of feathers.

Blaze caught up with him panting beneath the shadow of the escaping bird. "Not as easy as you thought?" she woofed.

Shep licked slobber from his jowls, and woofed between pants, "They're faster — *pant pant* — than they look — *pant pant* —"

"You're more of a rabbitter than a bird dog," Blaze said. "Come with me."

Shep followed Blaze through the alleys and copied her actions. If she sniffed a crevice, Shep's nose was on that spot the next heartbeat. Blaze explained that most of the rabbits were escaped pets, and thus were easy prey. "If you can find them," she woofed, grinning.

Shep drew the scents of the street into his nose. He

smelled each nuance of odor: the particular scent of the pool of water beneath a plastic sheet, indicating that it was three suns old; the stinging, sweet reek of a rotted piece of fruit; and the warm breath of life — a rabbit. It huddled, heart racing, only a stretch away under a stumpy palm tree.

Shep sank to his paws, chest to stone, and crept forward. He spotted all of the rabbit's possible escape routes: forward, into the street; back down the alley; it wouldn't come toward him, and it couldn't scamper away from him because there was a wall. *The rabbit will go for the street.*

Shep barked to scare it out from under the bush. The rabbit bolted for the street as Shep had planned. He sprang over the bush and landed on the creature's back. With a single bite of his powerful jaws, the rabbit fell still.

Shep dropped the little animal and stood panting over it. He felt that warmth running through him again — not the blind fear and rage of fighting or the weighty glow of being the alpha, but a strength from deep within. Like he was doing what his body was meant to do.

"You feel it, don't you?" Blaze woofed. She'd crept up beside him. "That fire under your fur? It's what I felt herding my beasts at the farm, what my man brought out in me." She sniffed his scruff. "I can smell that fire in you now. You're *alive.*"

Shep did feel alive, more alive than he'd ever felt before. And this made him terribly sad. He'd been so happy with his boy — was that happiness a lie? Blaze's man had brought out the fire in her. *Why didn't the boy bring out my fire?*

"What's wrong?" Blaze woofed, head tilted. "You seemed so happy a heartbeat ago."

Shep licked his jowls and pushed that terrible trail of thought from his mind. "I am happy," he said. "Let's do some more hunting."

Blaze grinned and waved her tail. "That's my hero," she yipped.

Shep picked up his rabbit and followed her down the street.

As they hunted, Blaze's banter changed from tips on finding rabbits to other advice. "Your team should warn the pack about water lizards," she woofed. "I saw one skulking across the street, following a wild dog who tried to bite it."

"Water lizards can leave the water?" Shep asked, scratching at what he swore was a white tail under a heap of garbage.

Then her last woofs registered like a Car to the skull. He stood slowly. "Did you say wild dog?" he barked. "Why didn't you get me? It could have attacked. There could be more!"

"You were out of the den, in one of your meetings, not around," Blaze yipped over her tail, as if it were nothing to see a wild dog. "I told Callie about it," she woofed. "Don't tell me she didn't tell you."

Shep didn't answer; his mind raced. The wild dogs had crossed the canal. The wild dogs were nearby. And Callie hadn't told him.

They found another rabbit, but Shep was so distracted he could barely get a claw on it before it scuttled deep under an overturned metal box. They returned to the den with the one carcass, exhausted. The other hunters hadn't had much better luck and every dog went to bed with a grumbling belly.

At the meeting that night, Shep confronted Callie about the wild dog.

She startled at his question. "Yes, Blaze told me," Callie answered, her bark wavering.

"And you didn't tell me?" Shep snarled.

"To be honest, I forgot," she woofed, sounding tired. "Who knows if it was a wild dog or just another lost pet? We have bigger problems."

"What could be bigger than wild dogs?" Shep barked, hysterical. "Have you forgotten what happened in the kibble den?"

Callie flattened her ears and lowered her tail. "How could you ask me that?" she growled. "No, I haven't," she continued, "but we have new problems, like starving and injured dogs."

"We deemed it a minor annoyance," Higgins snuffled. "And we figured, smelling as you've become so — grr, *close* to Blaze, she would have told you herself."

"I alerted the defense team," yipped Virgil humbly. "We've been on an extra alert watch for strange dogs."

Shep stared into the muzzles of each dog. They'd all known, and none had told him. "Aren't I the alpha of this pack?" he growled. "Shouldn't everything be run by me?"

Callie cocked her head. "Why are you so concerned about being alpha all of a sudden?" she snarled. "I thought we were a team."

"Well, then act like it, instead of letting me find out about something this important suns after it happens!"

"Fine," Callie snapped. "You want to hear about things, here you go." She rattled off all the problems facing the pack. Dogs were dying of serious injuries Boji hadn't the faintest scent of how to fix. Food was scarce. The hunters weren't killing enough kibble.

Higgins sat tall as if bracing for battle. "In my humble opinion, I don't smell why we're searching for new dogs at all. We can't even feed the ones we've rescued."

Honey sprang to her paws, ears and tail flat. "These dogs are trapped! Desperate! We're their only hope!" She was barking so loud every dog in the den had to have heard her.

Shep knew it wouldn't be popular among a pack full of rescues to inform them that their leaders were abandoning the effort. But what about food?

"We won't stop rescuing entirely," Callie woofed. "But we need to cut back on the number of dogs doing it and retrain them as hunters."

"You've already taken three," Honey whined.

Fuzz, however, purred and nodded his pointy head.

Virgil raised his snout. "I should report that I've heard dogs barking about this group," he woofed. "Seems that some in the pack are confused as to who's the leader."

"What does that matter?" yapped Higgins. "If there's one leader or a hundred, it shouldn't matter so long as the den's safe and there's kibble."

"But there isn't kibble, and there was another rat attack last night." Callie sighed, then shook herself, nose to tail. "Would it help, you think, to have Shep make announcements after each meeting?" She wasn't looking at Shep, but rather at Higgins and Virgil.

"Shouldn't *I* be the one making that decision?" Shep growled.

"Fine," Callie snapped. "Do you want to make a nightly speech?"

Shep looked at the little girldog who stood fiercely at his paws. She looked beyond tired, like she hadn't slept in suns.

"When was the last time you took a nap?" Shep asked quietly.

Callie's stance sagged. "I don't remember." She sat down, then began to scratch limply at her ear. "How long since we came to this den?"

"Too long," yapped Higgins.

"If you think nightly barks will help, I'm willing to try," Shep snuffled.

"Good," sighed Callie. "Tonight, we should also put to the pack whether to expand our food hunt to plants. I can tally the vote."

"Plants?" woofed Higgins, screwing up his little furface with disgust.

"Yes," answered Callie. "I think we could find some edible

plants. There's a plant that grows in the verge near the canal that's very crisp and full of nice watery juice. And I think we should let the pack decide, since they're the ones who are going to have to eat it."

"But they'll never agree," whined Shep. Just the thought of all those dogs barking *"Yay, plants!"* or *"Not until the slobber has dried on my dead jowls!"* set his belly groaning.

"Agree or no," woofed Callie, "isn't that the kind of pack you started?"

Shep thought about how much he regretted forcing the pack to let the cat join them; he should have let every dog vote on that decision. But the pack had been so small then. He could have guessed every dog's vote before they made it; he would have known what to say to make the idea appeal to each of them. Now, after so many suns and so many new rescues, he didn't even know how many dogs lived in the boat, let alone their opinions. Leaving any decision open to a vote was like chasing a rabbit through water in the dark — he had no idea what he'd end up with.

The rest of the leaders were waiting for him to woof. "Fine," he groaned. However fur-raising the prospect of letting the entire pack vote was, Shep knew it was the right thing to do.

Shep barked for order that night. It was steamy inside the den and several dogs had to be howled in from where they lounged in the cool evening breeze on the plaza. Once every dog was inside, Shep put the plant issue out for a vote. In a heartbeat, all the dogs were barking and yowling, some simply yelping out of nerves. Shep and the defense team used every dominance trick they knew to get the pack quiet again.

Shep turned to Callie, who sat beside him. "I think that's a 'no' to plants."

Callie nodded her snout. "Let them get hungry enough," she woofed. "They'll be begging for plants in a few suns."

Blaze found Shep after the meeting. "What was that vote nonsense about?" she yipped as they walked to the lower level.

"That was a pack making a decision," he growled, tired and not in the mood for a fight.

"I smell you're not happy with the results?" Blaze said, stepping back.

"It doesn't matter if I'm happy," Shep barked. "It's the pack's decision." He pulled himself into their den room and curled up in the corner. "Callie thinks they'll agree to eating plants once they're hungry enough."

"You're the alpha. Why not just tell the pack they're going to eat plants?" Blaze woofed, following him. "Why all this playing around with voting?"

"Because that's how it's done." Shep wished he had a better retort.

"That's not how it's done where I come from," Blaze grumbled. "On the beast farm, the master whistles, and the dog obeys."

"Enough with the beast farm," Shep snapped. "We're not on the farm, there are no men, and no beasts."

Blaze's eyes were wide and her ears were flat on her head. "You don't need to remind me of *that*, hero."

Shep sighed — he hadn't meant to snap at her. Of course things would have been easier if he'd just howled that they were eating plants and that was the end of it. But he was also glad that the pack made the decision. Now, they had only themselves to blame for the lack of plant kibble — if such a thing existed — and when it was offered to them later, they might give it a try. If he'd just forced it on them, they might have revolted. Shep recalled when his boy tried to shove bitter pills down his throat and how angry he'd been and how much of a betrayal it'd felt like. The last thing Shep wanted was to have a boat full of dogs feeling that way toward him.

"I'm no dog's master," he woofed to Blaze. "We're all equals in this pack."

Blaze snorted, and curled up in the opposite corner to sleep.

CHAPTER 12
A CHAMPION IS BORN

Though Shep was eager to hunt again, over the next few suns he had to devote most heartbeats to helping the defense team ward off an onslaught of Outsiders. Whether it was the concentration of food in the kibble room, or the fact that most of the pack loitered in the shade Outside every sun because it was too hot inside the boat — whatever the reason, other animals had decided that it was a good time to sneak in and cause problems.

Rat attacks were followed by an infestation of bugs the size of Shep's paw. Shep's first plan was to have the big dogs sniff out the insects, then get Daisy and Waffle to chase the bugs into the open where the others could help squash them. This turned out to be a more disgusting plan than he'd anticipated, as the bugs exploded into piles of goo when bitten. Plus, Mooch, Panzer, and Paulie were afraid of the shiny, scuttling invaders.

A few old timers who weren't assigned to a team saw the big dogs retching and cringing, and asked if they could help with the bug hunt.

"We all would love to eat some insects," yipped an old timer Chihuahua named ChaCha.

"Please!" groaned Shep as he scraped bug guts off his tongue with his teeth. "Eat them all!"

The old timers hobbled and hacked their way through the den in pursuit of their antennae-ed prey. A weepy-eyed poodle named Mr. Pickles nearly choked on one victim. He came sputtering out from under a broken chair with a huge smile on his jowls wheezing, "The old pickle's all right!"

All the old timers seemed grateful to have a job to do.

"It's nice to dig your paws into something," ChaCha yipped. "Most suns, I feel about as useful as a broken collar."

When Fuzz heard about the bug hunt, he also offered a paw. The last thing Shep wanted was the meower hissing at him, but Virgil agreed that Fuzz could help before Shep could so much as woof. Much to Shep's surprise, Fuzz seemed as happy as the old timers to scamper after the insects.

"Bugs taste crunchy-good," Fuzz growled, a thin stick of

leg protruding from his short jowls. "Big dogs not under-stand what food they miss."

Shep loved being around all the old timers. He couldn't help but wag his tail as he watched them frisk about like pups, yelping "Here's another one!" and "This scrapper's try-ing to fly!" It reminded him of how nice it'd been when the pack was smaller and less of a weight around his neck. Back when he could just *play*. Back when he was just another dog, and not some all-knowing alpha or mystical Champion. Shep was almost sorry when the last of the disgusting creatures was gulped down.

The next morning, a water lizard was sighted sunning itself on the ramp to the canal. The defense team managed to scare it off with a group barking attack; however, for the rest of the sun, no dog wanted to leave the den for fear of being eaten. By midsun, the mob was moaning about how thirsty they were. Shep thought it might help if the defense team dragged one of the water boats closer to the den, but the team jerked the hull too hard and the boat broke. Water spilled out in a torrent onto the sizzling street. Every dog in the den howled with anger at the loss.

"Now they'll ration water in addition to kibble," one dog growled.

Sure enough, that evening, Higgins told every dog they were limited to five snoutfuls of water a sun until the next rain. Shep spent that night Outside with Dover, hiding from the pack's hateful looks. *Like I* wanted *to spill the water*, he grumbled to himself.

Then there were the snakes. Huge diamond-backed ropes like the one Shep had uncovered, narrow things like shoe-strings, snakes of every size and color lurked under stones or dropped out of trees. Most were harmless. But one bit a pup on the paw; the poor girldog was dead in a heartbeat. The attack got every dog barking.

"What's the defense team doing to get rid of the snakes?" one dog bayed.

"Forget the defense team," another grumbled. "Where's our great alpha? Why hasn't he killed the snakes?"

It was as if to distract themselves from their hunger and thirst, they complained about the snakes, or the bats, or the felines caterwauling in the street at night.

"How can my pups get any sleep with all that racket?" one dam whined.

As the griping of some pack members swelled to a dull roar, others' woofs were devoted entirely to the repetition of the Storm Shaker legend. Shep heard it mumbled while he was lapping up his water ration, while he was moving through the stairwell, and during his shift guarding the entries on the crushed floor. Though he still cringed every time he heard it, a small part of him appreciated the silly story. It reminded him that at least at one point, he'd done something heroic. And it was better than a complaint.

The nightly meetings were taken over with whining from one end of the den to the other. Shep's announcements consisted of merely acknowledging every dog's fears and telling them it would all be fine. Shep worried, however, that his barks provided less comfort to the pack than they once had.

"When's the alpha going to start showing these scavengers who's boss?" one dog barked at the end of Shep's speech.

The next night, it was more than one dog barking about an alpha. "If you can't keep the pack safe, maybe we should start scenting for a new leader!"

The third night, there were several dogs bellowing about sniffing out a new alpha. Shep scanned the pack and scented for any strange odors. He identified several dogs who smelled anxious, at least more anxious than the general crowd. Shep marked those scents in his memory, then stood tall.

"I'll have no more barking about a new alpha!" he snapped. "Callie and I and the other pack leaders are keeping every dog as safe and as well fed as possible. If you have ideas we haven't tried, please come tell us. Now back to your dens!"

As the dogs dispersed, he followed the scent of the alpha-barkers. He traced their track into the old food room, which was dark as death and smelled of old kibble gone to rot.

"They're never going to submit," one dog — *Bernie?* — woofed. "They know we're not seriously going to challenge them."

"Why do you think that?" growled a girldog who sounded a lot like Blaze.

Shep couldn't believe his ears. He took a careful, quiet scent. He'd been right — it *was* Blaze.

"If a few more of the big dogs join us," Blaze continued, "we won't have to challenge them. Shep and Virgil can't protect the yappers."

Shep smelled that there were two others in the room besides Blaze and Bernie. He dropped down from the hall into the food room.

"How could you?" he growled. "And why would you?"

Three of the dogs leapt away from Shep, hitting the cabinets lining the front wall. Shep could smell their fear and shock. Blaze smelled only of herself.

"I can't believe it took you this long to find us," she snarled.

"*Why*, Blaze?" Shep whimpered.

Blaze moved closer to him, her scent overwhelming his nose. "I'm doing this for you, you big fuzz head." She licked his nose. "Once the pack overthrows the yappers, it'll be clear for you to take control."

Shep snapped at Blaze's snout and she shied back, confused.

"We've been barking about you being alpha for suns," she snarled. "I figured you just needed some help getting going."

"I don't *want* to be alpha," Shep growled, "not in that way, not alone. That's not the kind of pack I run. I thought you understood that."

"The pack you run?" Blaze yipped. "If you run the pack, why is this even a discussion? Stop pretending that the dogs are voting or doing anything other than following your —

not the yappers' — rules. Dogs need an alpha. Be the leader you know you are."

Shep turned his muzzle to the three cringers near the front wall. "Get back to your dens."

"No!" barked Blaze. "This is our chance!" She leapt out of the rear door-hole, scrambled up to the hall, and bounded into the main den.

Shep chased after her and tackled her mid-stride. Blaze shot him a look full of hurt, like this was his betrayal and not her own.

"Why are you fighting this?" she growled. "Stop hiding behind those cringers!" She rose and began to circle Shep.

"I'm not hiding!" Shep snapped. "We are a *team*. But I guess you can't understand that."

"Team." Blaze spat the bark from her jowls as if it were poison. "There's the alpha, and there are the followers. Your idea of a team is a joke. Who's really making the decisions? Is it you, or is it Callie?"

Shep glanced at the crowd of dogs forming around them. This was suddenly about more than just whether Blaze was right or wrong. Blaze could break the fragile peace that held this pack together.

Shep stepped back. "I won't fight you, Blaze," he woofed. "But you're wrong. This pack isn't run by an alpha; it's run by all the dogs. We all play our parts. If you don't like it, you're free to go."

Blaze growled, raising her hackles. She glared at Shep. "That's not how dogs are meant to live. We need one leader to guide us. This dream of all dogs having a say, it's just that: a dream." She swung her snout at the crowd of dogs. Their numbers were hidden by darkness, but Shep could smell that the whole of the pack was there, ears open.

Blaze turned to them and continued, "You dogs, you can smell I'm right. We need leadership. What do we know of life without our humans? We need a dog to help guide us. And if Shep won't be that dog, then I say we smell out another!"

Several dogs barked their approval. Then some others howled that Shep *was* such a leader. Shep smelled anger in the air. A dog snarled, then Shep heard fighting near the rear of the boat. It was all coming apart. How could he pull things back together?

The lights flared on.

Standing between Shep and Blaze were Oscar, Ginny, and several pups. Oscar howled a strange high-pitched yowl, which was answered by dogs from all corners of the den.

"Followers of Shep!" Oscar bayed. "We know the true lineage of our leader. He is the Champion of the Great Wolf, come to save us in this time of need! He is the Storm Shaker, the true leader! As the Great Wolf shines above us, as the Silver Moon crosses the sky, we know that Shep will shine true and lead us through these times of darkness. As Lassie guided dogs to humans, so Shep will guide us when our humans abandon us."

"All praise Shep!" howled Odie.

"Shep!" innumerable voices barked. His name rang throughout the den.

Blaze looked at Shep as much in confusion as in anger. Shep looked back at her blankly, not sure what to do. But he didn't have to do anything. Oscar's followers stepped forward, each crawling before Shep and licking his paws. The rest of the pack — confused, scared — followed their lead, and came cringing before Shep.

Frozen there in the unnaturally bright light, with strange dogs bearing their bellies to him, Shep felt just as he had on that first night after his family abandoned him: powerless, scared, and faced with a world he did not understand. Who were these dogs, so willingly submitting to him? Who was this bold pup standing beside him, leading a pack of his own, yet looking up at Shep with adoring eyes? Who was Shep to accept that adoration? This parade of submission? *I am not the Great Wolf's Champion*, he thought, almost as a reminder to himself. His teeth chattered under his jowls.

When the last dog had finished licking Shep's claws, Shep tried to sniff Blaze out, but she was lost amidst the scents of the other dogs. He escaped up the table-ramp to the meeting room, where Callie sat alone in the darkness.

"Did you hear what happened?" Shep woofed.

"I heard it," Callie said.

"What was Oscar thinking?" Shep asked, as much to himself as Callie. "What gave that little pup the fur to jump into a fight?"

"I did," Callie barked flatly.

Shep stepped back. "You?" he yipped.

"I've known about Oscar's club since it started," Callie barked, her voice tired. "It's grown, as I guess you now know. The dogs liked hearing the stories, and they spread like fleas throughout the pack."

"But you know I hate those stories," Shep woofed. "I'm not the Great Wolf's Champion. From the beginning, I didn't want dogs telling stories that I was in any way related to the Great Wolf. I want the pack to follow *me*, not some myth. I want to be my own dog."

"At what cost?" Callie asked. "The pack was set to tear itself apart. You heard them. Blaze was scratching at an itch many dogs have been feeling. You either had to fight her, or find some other way." Callie licked her front paw. "I knew you wouldn't fight her, so I found another way."

"But now what?" Shep woofed. "What will the pack think when they find out I'm just another dog?"

"I guess we'll choke on that bone when we come to it."

Shep lay down. He wasn't sure what to say. Callie was right; something had to be done in that heartbeat, and Shep had frozen. But now what? How was he supposed to act every sun, now that he'd been officially unveiled as the Champion of the Great Wolf? Even thinking the idea made his fur itch. *What will the Great Wolf think of me now, pretending to be what I so clearly am not?*

"I wish you'd woofed with me about this," Shep said, finally.

"What would you have said?" Callie lay facing him, but her eyes stared up at the window. The sky was cloudy.

147

"I don't want to be their Champion," Shep whimpered.

"It's not just about what you want anymore."

Shep lay there in the dark. Callie was right — again. As always. He knew that the pack mattered more than he did. He remembered how he'd felt facing down Kaz. He'd been ready then to sacrifice himself for the group. But the pack itself had been small; he'd known each dog's scent. Now, the pack was so large, he had no idea who was new from one sun to the next. Was he really ready to sacrifice himself for all these dogs, these strangers? Was this really who he wanted to be?

As Shep rose to his paws, he thought about saying something to Callie, something about how much he appreciated her help, or how much he needed her as a partner. But he said nothing. He left her in the dark, staring up at the blank face of the clouds, and took the back staircase-hole to the crushed floor and Out into the night.

Dover sat beneath his boat, as he did every night. Shep joined him, as had become his own habit.

"Hear the ruckus?" Shep grunted, sitting beside the old timer.

"Heard it," Dover woofed, "but not sure what to make of it."

"Pack's still holding together," Shep said.

"By a dewclaw," Dover added, looking at Shep with his deep brown eyes. Then he smiled. "But that's better than most could do with a pack of this size, facing dangers no dog has smelled since before the first collar."

They sat together in the dark, feeling the breeze ruffle the fur on their backs. When sleep came, Shep curled next to Dover and the old dog rested his snout on the younger dog's scruff.

"You're doing good, pup," Dover snuffled. "Real good."

CHAPTER 13
HUNGER PANGS

The next morning, as Shep lapped up his drink ration, he paused to examine the muzzle reflected in the water. His jowls were flecked with white hairs, and his eyes seemed to have shrunken under his brow. The dog in the water looked worn-out. *What's happening to me?* Shep wondered.

"Shep!" Oscar cried as he bounded up to him. "I can't tell you how amazing last night was." His ears were up and tail was wagging. "Getting to stand next to you, in front of the whole club was even more exciting than watching you fight those wild dogs! Odie said he thought that we kind of looked alike, like maybe I could be your pup. Isn't that the best-smelling thing ever?"

Shep felt awkward even meeting Oscar's eyes. "We look nothing alike."

Oscar's tail drooped slightly, but kept wagging. "Well, he didn't say *exactly* alike, just maybe something noble about the snout?" Oscar waved his little nose in the air, demonstrating its proportions for Shep.

Shep didn't know what else to say, so he said the only thing on his mind. "Pup, I don't like that story you made up. I don't like all these dogs in your club thinking I'm something I'm not."

If Shep had torn Oscar's tail off, the pup probably would have looked less hurt.

The woofs trembled as they fell from his jowls. "But last night — I thought . . ." His eyes were wide, and his ears hung limp around his muzzle. "I only wanted to help you, like Callie said. Didn't my story and my club help you?"

Shep sagged into a sit next to the pup. "It's not that you didn't help," he said, "it's just that the Great Wolf, he really means something to me."

Oscar's tail began to wave and wriggle. "He means so much to me, too, Shep!" he barked. "When Callie told me that story while the wave was crashing all around us, all I could think of was you fighting that whole pack of wild dogs and Zeus and how much that was just like the Great Wolf and the Black Dog. And then when we told Odie that story together, it suddenly all piled together for me, about you and the Great Wolf and being his Champion. I mean, how else could you have done all that incredible stuff? The Great Wolf *must* have smelled how much you were like him and made you into his Champion!"

Shep shook his head. "Oscar, you really believe that? About the hairs and the tears?"

Oscar crinkled his nose. "Ginny added that stuff in," he woofed. "Do you not like those parts? Because I thought the story didn't need anything more than just what really happened, but Ginny said it needed 'fluff and fancy-ing,' whatever that meant. She also stuck on that bit about Lassie." Oscar panted. "I don't even know who Lassie is." He grinned at Shep and wagged his tail. "It's hard to run a club, you know?"

Shep did know, better than any dog. But he didn't feel right barking about that kind of thing with a pup. Particularly when the pup was running a club whose very existence made Shep's fur crawl. Woofing about things with Dover was one thing; confiding in Oscar was another bag of treats entirely.

Shep stood up. "Oscar, I'm sorry if you're having troubles, but that club is a burr you put in your own fur. All I wanted to bark is that I wish you'd have left me and the Great Wolf out of it." Shep took a final lap of water. "The Great Wolf is my hero. Don't you understand how that makes him special to me?"

"I do," Oscar grunted. His tail was so far between his legs, its tip dragged in the dirt. "Don't *you* understand that you're *my* hero, Shep?" The pup loped away from him and disappeared inside the boat.

Shep sighed; he felt like a pile of scat. *Why couldn't I have just wagged my tail and walked away?* What kind of dog was he, to be tearing the squeaker out of the pup's toy? He was doing everything wrong. As he trotted out to begin his hunt, several pack members crouched to let him pass, a mixture of fear and awe on their muzzles. Shep broke into a run and only stopped when he could no longer scent the boat.

He decided to set small goals for himself, to make the hunt even more exciting. He would bring in the most prey that any hunter had caught in one sun. He found a metal box in an alley, heavy enough to keep out scavengers, and flipped it over: He would hide his prey inside.

By midsun, he'd downed two rabbits and a squirrel. He chased a chipmunk into a ruined den and smelled an interesting, musky scent. It was a ferret, still trapped in its cage. Shep pawed the cage and the nasty weasel spat and scratched at Shep's claw. Its beady eyes betrayed a vicious intelligence. The ferret was not going to give in that easily.

Shep found the door to the cage and bent it open with his teeth. "There you go," he woofed to the ferret. "Now we can fight fair."

The weasel considered Shep for a heartbeat, then sprang for the open cage door and squeezed its way through. It smiled at Shep; they both knew what was coming.

The ferret bolted across the floor, its long body humping along the stone. Shep scrambled after it, heart racing. The weasel wriggled into a tiny hole in the corner, thinking Shep couldn't follow. Shep jammed his paw into the hole and ripped the sheet of paper-stone from the wallboards. The ferret squealed and dove at Shep's paw. Shep swept down with his jaws, barely missing the cunning creature's head.

The weasel leapt at Shep's jowls, and Shep rolled the thing onto its back. The ferret snapped and clawed at Shep's snout. He could barely land a tooth before the thing had its head out of the way. Then Shep mashed the weasel's chest with his massive paw and caught its head in his jaws. The fight was over.

Shep snuck into the den through the stairwell and dropped his four kills in the kibble room while Higgins was fussing with rations in the back corner. The only dog who saw him was Snoop, who had been assigned to help Higgins with kibble distribution. He barely got in a "Hey-Shep-how-ya'-doin'?" before Shep slipped back into the stairwell and out into the evening.

When the time came for the nightly meeting, he forced himself back inside, though he'd been tracking a cunning rodent through a maze of rubble. He sat in the shadows and let the other leaders bark. He braved the glazed gazes of his adoring throng to give his nightly speech, then escaped the cramped walls of the boat into the clear night.

Each sun, Shep sought out more challenging animals to hunt, things that would really test his skills. He caught an iguana easily — they were half-asleep whenever they were lounging in the sun. Birds were more difficult. Shep practiced sprinting up and down an alley. Once his speed was near that of a rabbit, he focused on timing his leap and snap-bite. Then he went after his first bird.

It was a lithe white bird on long black legs with a thin orange snout. It moved slowly through a brackish puddle behind a demolished den. Shep kept downwind of the squawker, low to the ground and hidden by bramble. The bird flicked its head away; this was his chance. He exploded from the hedge, paws flying over the grass. The bird barely had time to register his existence before needing to flap open its lovely fans of wing. It slapped the air and lifted off the ground. Shep sprang up and snapped his fangs around its slender neck. He landed with the bird hanging limp from his jaws.

He sought out more dangerous prey: huge rats with teeth the size of a pup's snout; small water lizards; a nasty old lizard that lived inside a green bowl of shell with a hard, snappy mouth and sharp, clawed paws. He fought all sizes of rodent — medium-sized ones with black muzzle masks and striped tails, white-faced ones that hung like fruit in trees, and once, near dusk, a huge bat whose leathery wings were studded with claws.

Shep even found a rodent-like thing encased in a hard, horny shell like a nut. The creature had a pointy nose, long ears, and a tiny, bony tail. The heartbeat it scented Shep, it began scratching furiously in the dirt. Shep hooked a claw on its shell just before it disappeared. He smelled lifeblood and fur under the shell, so he flipped the thing over and found its soft underbelly. The weird rodent became kibble in heartbeats.

Shep dragged what he could back to the boat, and always forced himself to sit through the nightly meetings. He made his customary speech to the pack as quickly as possible, then dashed back Out to the hunt.

Several suns into his hunting spree, a thunderstorm rolled over the city. Shep decided to take the morning off. He pulled himself into the meeting room, which the bulk of the pack avoided, and curled up in a corner to wait out the storm. Before he could so much as close his eyes, he heard a girldog woof his name — well, one of his names.

"The Storm Shaker is Out saving other dogs, sweet snout," a dam snuffled to her pup. "That's why he left us his Voice."

Shep shot to his paws and dropped down into the hallway below. The dam was startled, and her pup hid beneath her flank.

"Storm Shaker!" she cried. "Be a good pup, Shag," she woofed to the pup. "You wanted to smell the Storm Shaker, and here he is."

The pup peeked out at Shep, then ducked back under his mother.

The dam licked her pup, then smiled at Shep. "He's just shy. Seven suns old this morning!"

"Oh," Shep woofed. "Congratulations." He hadn't barked one-on-one with another dog in . . . how many suns? The woofs felt strange on his tongue. "What did you say about a Voice?"

The dam's tail drooped. "Is this some sort of test? Grr, let me smell if I can remember it exactly." She cocked her head. "Oh, yes."

The Storm Shaker set out to complete his work of rescuing animals trapped by the storm. He worked from when dawn's tails first wagged in the sky until the last of the sun's light faded, and his packmates struggled alongside him.

As the pack gathered more dogs, the Storm Shaker realized that he could not both continue his mission and lead the pack. He noticed a young pup sitting quietly at the edge of the crowd, looking up at the Storm Shaker with an intense gaze. The Storm Shaker approached the pup.

"Why do you not play with your packmates?" the Storm Shaker asked.

"I want to be like you," the pup replied.

"Then you shall help me," the Storm Shaker barked.

The pup was small, and could not tear a door from its hinges or dig through a sodden wall. But the pup was smart, and his bark was loud and clear. The Storm Shaker said to the pup, "You will spread the story of the Storm Shaker, and in that way lead this pack. By hearing my story, all dogs may learn to be free and live in peace."

"Stop!" Shep cried.

The dam swallowed her woofs. "Did I get something wrong?"

Shep pushed past her, his nose on Oscar's scent. It led him to a corner of the main den near the windowed back wall of the boat. Oscar sat on a ripped pillow, yipping quietly with Odie.

"Might the Storm Shaker have a word with his Voice?" Shep growled.

Oscar looked up at him, surprised. He waved his snout and Odie trotted away.

"So you heard the new story," Oscar woofed, his bark flat.

"I thought I made it clear that I didn't like these stories." Shep tried to keep his woofs quiet.

Oscar sat taller. "You made it very clear." His bark broke every few yips into a whimper. "But all the dogs wondered where you were. They kept asking me, 'Where's the Storm Shaker? Why isn't he ever in the den?' They felt like they'd been abandoned all over again. They needed a story to make them feel better. To make them feel like you didn't *hate* them." He spat the last woofs out.

Shep was again stunned to silence. Oscar trembled in his stiff sit, his snout lifted proudly, his eyes locked on Shep's own. The pup had grown in the moon-cycle Shep had known him. He fit his ears and paws a bit better, and he didn't trip when he walked. His gaze possessed a depth dug out by all the adventures and ordeals he'd experienced since they'd met in that dim hallway what seemed like cycles ago, like another world entirely.

"I don't hate you, Oscar," Shep snuffled, finally.

Oscar trembled even harder, as if fighting with his own muscles, then shook with one enormous shiver and sagged. "It sure feels like you hate us," he grunted.

"I'm Out hunting for food," Shep woofed, though he knew that was only half the truth, maybe less than half.

Oscar pulled his sit straighter. "Do you have a different story you want me to tell? I'll say whatever you want." His tail gave a feeble wag and a smile curled his jowls. "Working together, I'm sure we could come up with some really good-smelling stuff." He leaned toward Shep, and his tail wagged harder.

Shep shrank back. He didn't want more stories, or different stories; he wanted *no* stories. Why didn't Oscar understand? The pup was so hopeful, so happy. He looked at Shep the way he had back in the kibble den, after the wave. He looked at Shep like Shep was a hero. But Shep didn't feel like that dog anymore. He didn't want to lead; he didn't want to be a hero — he wanted to be left alone to hunt. Everything was so clear and simple when he was hunting. There was the hunter and the hunted; there was a beginning and an end. He had to get back to that world in as few heartbeats as possible.

"I'm not good at stories, pup," he groaned. He turned and padded away from Oscar as quickly as the crowded den allowed.

He stepped into the stairwell, ready to escape, and bumped snouts with Honey.

"They've killed a cat, Shep!" she barked hysterically. "A *cat!*" She waved her muzzle at Fuzz.

Fuzz cowered beneath Honey's belly like a shadow. Over the suns, he'd cleaned his fur of most of its mats, and now he looked as his name implied — he was a black cloud of fur. Faint stripes ran throughout his coat, and a shock of white blazed at his chest. His green eyes were wide open, and he scanned the empty passage around them like the hunters were already on his trail and fast approaching.

Shep had known this sun would come. In fact, he was surprised that it'd taken the hunting teams until now to catch a cat, though felines were tougher prey to catch than rodents and lizards.

Shep licked Honey's nose — he'd always liked the girldog. "What can I say?" he woofed. "Cats are prey to most dog's noses."

Honey's tail pressed even farther between her hind legs. She cocked her head. "But I thought you wanted to save the cats," she whimpered. "Wasn't that part of our plan?"

Shep waved his tail, then gave Fuzz a friendly snort. In reply, the cat swatted at Shep's nose.

"Things are bad right now, Honey," Shep woofed quietly. He had only the loosest bite on the actual current status of the pack, but he was sure that things remained as bad as ever. "The pack is near starving. If a hunting team's brought in a cat, how can I tell these dogs not to eat it?"

Honey pulled away from him, her eyes cold. "What about when they bring in a dead pup? A dead yapper? What will you say then? 'It was dead. How can I stop them?'" All the usual joy had been drained from her bark. "I thought you were serious about saving all pets in need." She flicked her tail and Fuzz climbed onto her shoulders.

"What *are* you serious about, Shep? What do you really believe in?"

She hurried away from him into the dark of the lower level.

Shep let her woofs rattle around his skull. He wanted to tell Honey that he agreed with her, that he didn't want the pack to eat cats, but that it was easy to say such things when a dog was only making decisions for himself. He wondered if she'd have the fur to tell the whole pack that they shouldn't eat cats, instead of running to him. He certainly didn't have the fur to bark such a thing. He couldn't even tell Oscar to stop making up lies. Why did it feel like all his friends hated him?

Shep sniffed out Callie in an empty room inside the bottom floor of the boat. She was huddled in the dim light from a small lamp in the wall, with several piles of weeds set out before her.

"Honey hates me," Shep woofed. "Oscar hates me."

"I told you not to start in with that cat stuff," Callie said, her jowls frilled with green leaves. "And Oscar loves you. You're just too stuffed-up to smell it." Callie chewed and her jowls curled with each bite. She continued, "I've been looking for you for the past few suns. You dash away the heartbeat the meeting is over at night, and there's never a whiff of you in the boat. Virgil told me you even asked him to reassign your guard post. Where've you been?"

"Hunting," Shep yipped, leaving it at that. "You're not seriously eating plants now, are you?" He sniffed one of the piles. It smelled bitter and bright, and a faint trace of urine coated at least one of the leaves.

Callie spat out the plants from her mouth. "Yes, I'm seriously eating plants." She slapped the silver paw in the wall next to her and a thin trickle of water dribbled out. She lapped up the water, then spat it from her jowls and smacked the silver paw again to shut off the flow. "Those last ones were terrible, but I've found at least three kinds of plants that will work as kibble."

She pushed a plant toward Shep. He sniffed it — green, water, a hint of dirt and human chemicals. "You want me to eat this?"

Callie waved her tail. "It's good," she woofed.

Shep licked up the leaf and crunched it between his teeth. "Good" seemed the wrong word; more like "edible" with a dash of "if desperate."

"It's fine," he barked, choking the last bit down. "But a dog would have to eat a bush full of these to feel full."

"Full is not the issue," Callie replied, sweeping a pile of pointy, dark green leaves in front of her. "Alive is what I'm working for."

Shep kept her company as she gnawed on the fleshy shoots. Callie had changed over the moon-cycles. The brightness, the excitement that used to radiate out of her was gone. There was no joy in her eyes, no wag to her tail. She seemed to be slogging ahead out of sheer stubbornness.

"How about you and me run away together?" Shep snuffled.

Callie raised her snout and smiled. Her tail even waved slightly. "Race off to that mystical warm, dry den filled with gravy-laced kibble and velveteen beds?"

"I think we can make it there," he woofed, "just the two of us."

"And if the others follow?" Callie yipped.

"Let 'em try," Shep woofed.

Callie panted. Then her eyes changed — the sparkle went out completely. She began to cough and wheeze. She dug her claws into the floor as hacking breaths wracked her tiny frame.

"Get — *cough* — Higgins!" she yelped.

She fell onto her side and began to writhe uncontrollably. Shep climbed out of the room, his heart pounding in his head. *Great Wolf, no! Not Callie! Please, no!*

He nearly fell over Higgins in the kibble den. "Callie!" Shep screamed. "She's sick!"

Higgins raced with Shep back to where Callie lay, still trembling. White foam leaked from her jowls. Bits of green flecked the spittle.

Higgins sniffed over the various piles. He was shivering and his tail was between his legs. "My snout," he whimpered. "I know nothing of plants." He sniffed the spittle and then the piles again. "I think it's this one, with the flowers. Get Boji."

Boji had no idea what to do, either. "Oh, dear," she whimpered, licking Callie's jowls. "Tastes bad."

She sniffed the silver paw, then turned it on. She nosed

Callie's muzzle under the flow. The water rinsed the foam and green bits away. Boji then forced Callie's jaws open with her paws so that the water spilled down her gullet.

"What are you doing?" Shep groaned.

"She needs to get this plant out of her," Boji barked. "I'm trying to make her spit it up."

Callie's eyelids split open and she began coughing violently. She threw up a sickly yellow puddle of foamy spit and leaves, then lay down and dropped into sleep.

Boji sniffed the puddle, and pronounced that this was all they could do for Callie. "She's got to fight whatever was in this herself."

Higgins trembled against the wall. "I told her not to start with these infernal plants," he grumbled. "But did she listen? No, never. Most stubborn dog I've ever smelled." He sounded miserable, like he'd just lost his only pup.

Boji and Higgins were scaring the fur off Shep's back. "But she'll be okay, right?" he barked. "Now that she's coughed up this plant, she'll get better. Right?"

He looked at Boji and Higgins, and they looked at each other.

Higgins coughed, then sat. "Let's hope so," he woofed.

Boji curled beside Callie, promising to get Higgins and Shep once Callie woke. Shep noticed that she was careful not to bark "if."

Higgins returned to counting kibbles in the storage room. Shep dragged himself into his old den on the ceiling. He'd not returned there since his fight with Blaze, hadn't so much as woofed hello to her in all those suns. He found her in the den, curled up in the darkness.

"The Champion returns," she woofed.

Shep padded closer to her. "Why did you challenge me?" he asked, sighing. "Why couldn't you just leave it alone?"

Blaze lifted her head. The dim light through the window was barely enough to show the outline of her muzzle. "I believe what I said," she barked. "We're lost without an alpha."

"The pack is fine," Shep said, feeling defensive and unsure exactly why. "We're managing."

"Oh, really?" Blaze raised her chest so that she was sitting eye to eye with Shep. "You've been spending your suns sniffing out the problems with the pack? Oh, no, wait: You've been scarce as a fresh bag of kibble. Did you know that Honey attacked some hunters who brought in a cat? Hulk and Virgil dragged her off one she'd gotten a good bite on. She was barking hysterically and snapping at any dog who came near her. She kept screaming, 'Where will it stop?'" Blaze licked her jowls. "This pack needs an alpha to tell it what's right and what's wrong, what makes you a good pack member and what will get you thrown out. Without that, we're two stretches away from becoming like this Black Dog that Oscar's little club keeps barking about, the one you fought."

"I didn't really fight him," Shep tried to explain. "The Black Dog and the Great Wolf is a story —"

"Right, well, Oscar keeps barking about you and some dog Zeus and your big battle," Blaze interrupted.

165

Shep startled at hearing his friend's name — his ex-friend's name. "Zeus was a real dog," Shep woofed. "My best friend. He turned against us during the storm." Shep looked up at the window, at the clouds bunched in the black. "He was scared. He didn't want to die. Or maybe it's just that he didn't want to fight for something and then lose."

"Standing up for what you believe in is hard." Blaze shuffled closer to Shep. "It hurt me to stand up to you in front of the pack. But I would do it again."

"It must be nice to know what you believe in," Shep woofed, lying down beside Blaze's paws.

Blaze panted softly, then stepped away from him and circled in the corner. "Stop feeling sorry for yourself," she said. "You could lead this pack if you believed in yourself half as much as this ragtag pack of crazy, confused pets does."

"And you, Blaze?" Shep woofed. "You wouldn't try to stop me?"

Blaze lifted her muzzle. "No, Shep," she said. "But I don't have to stop you. You've stopped yourself."

CHAPTER 14
RIPPLES ON THE SURFACE

At the first wag of dawn's tails, Shep was in Callie's den, sniffing her sleeping form.

Boji woke at the scent and nosed him away from Callie. "She needs rest," she woofed. "But I think she'll be all right."

"Thank the Great Wolf," Shep muttered.

"I thought you were he," woofed Boji, a smile on her jowls.

Shep panted lightly. "Well, I have this habit of thanking myself for everything that happens."

"Come back around midsun," Boji woofed. "Callie should be feeling better by then."

Shep spent the morning hunting along the back alleys near the boat. He didn't want to go too far, in case Callie needed him. He nearly missed catching a squirrel, he was so distracted. It was like reentering the pack for even a heart-beat had taken the bite out of his hunting skills.

Shep passed several other dogs, but ducked away from them. He dreaded the scent of his own pack — he felt like a coward. Maybe he needed to be the kind of leader Blaze wanted, the one reflected in Oscar's eyes. If he'd taken control from the beginning, maybe he could have made the pack into something great, and not simply a bunch of scared dogs waiting for masters who might never return. Maybe he could have kept this Storm Shaker craziness from taking hold like a worm in the lifeblood. Maybe he could have kept Callie from eating that plant.

No, he reminded himself, *there is no "controlling" Callie*. And what about the pack as a whole? If he couldn't handle one small — strong-willed and stone-headed, but singular and small — dog, how could he expect to have control over a whole pack? Was being an alpha anything more than an illusion?

Kaz had had control, if rampant fear could be called control. But she hadn't cared about being in charge. She led the wild dogs, but only because they all feared her. She herself had been fearless to her last breath. Was that what leadership was? Scaring everyone with your fearlessness? Ruling because no dog could smell what you might do next?

Shep gave himself a scratch behind the ears. He'd been right to work as a team, and to always share his power with the pack. Maybe he needed to listen to them more to get them to work together. Maybe the ideal leader was like a window, merely allowing the light of the pack to shine through him.

When the sun rose to its highest point, he returned to the den. He passed the kibble room to drop off the squirrel and noticed that the hunters had had better luck than usual. There was a healthy pile of dead rodents and lizards, and even a bag of kibble, by some small miracle. Higgins was busy gleefully calculating rations for the sun.

"It'll be more than a mouthful for each dog tonight, I'd wager!" he yipped, tail wagging.

Shep felt good, and then even better when he saw that Callie was awake and holding her head up as Boji licked her jowls.

"Thank the Great Wolf," he whimpered, crouching low to sniff her.

"Thank yourself," Callie said, her bark reduced to a wheeze. "If you hadn't been here —"

"But I was," Shep woofed, "and so was Boji, and now you're okay, which is all that matters."

Callie licked his nose. "Boji thinks I need rest."

"You do need rest," woofed Boji. "I can tell that you haven't slept in suns."

"I'm with Boji," Shep woofed. "You haven't been yourself. I miss my friend, the one who couldn't keep her tail from wagging."

Callie panted, then was wracked by a fit of coughing. "But the pack — *cough* — what about the food? Have you counted the new members yet? And there was a fight between a couple of the Yorkies about whether they should be forced to sleep in the same den when the other small dogs each got their own."

Shep hadn't heard about the fight with the Yorkies, and wasn't exactly sure he could pick out a Yorkie from any other yapper, but more importantly he hadn't known that Callie had been keeping track of all the new members. "Are you barking that you actually know how many dogs are in this pack?"

"Name and breed," she woofed. "Higgins needs to know so he can divide up the food."

"No wonder you haven't been sleeping," Shep yipped. "I'm beginning to feel like I haven't been pulling my weight."

"You're the muzzle the pack looks to," Callie woofed. "That's a tough enough job."

"At least I've slept," Shep snuffled.

"Well, you do get some perks as the muzzle." She smiled, then rested her head on her paws. "I feel like all these suns of not sleeping have finally caught up with me."

"I'll let you rest," Shep woofed.

Boji wagged her tail, letting him know he could go and that she would watch Callie. "I'll get you if she needs you," she woofed.

Shep decided that he should take over some of what Callie had been doing, starting with sniffing out how many new dogs had been recruited that morning. He caught Honey's scent near the entrance to one of the dens on the bottom level of the boat. She was curled up in the semidarkness, her den being in the floor, on the bottom-side of the boat.

"Hey, Honey," Shep barked. "I need to know how many dogs your team rescued this sun."

"That's easy," she snarled. "None."

Shep scented that Honey was angry, but not interested in a fight. She seemed to be seething in her own fur. "Did you find empty buildings? Dead dogs?" he woofed, wondering what might be troubling the girldog.

"We, and by 'we' I mean Fuzz and myself, since our team was gutted to fill the hunting ranks, didn't go out looking for any dogs. If this pack's willing to eat cats, then I'm not interested in bringing any more dogs into it to feed off my friends." Honey lifted herself and turned so that her back faced Shep. "Now leave us alone."

Shep scented for where Fuzz was. He smelled like he was under Honey.

"Where's Fuzz?" Shep woofed.

"Why do you care?" Honey snapped.

Shep stepped back, wary of how angry Honey — sweet, gentle, caring Honey — was. An angry dog was an unpredictable dog. "I care about Fuzz, Honey," he yipped. "I care about you, too."

"Really?" she growled. "I don't believe you. I believe that you want to be nice to everyone, but when the fur's on the line, you don't care."

Now she's being unfair, Shep thought. "I smell you're still angry that the pack ate a cat, and I'm sorry about that whole thing. But these dogs are hungry and the pack needs whatever food it can get." Shep was making a pronouncement on something; he felt strong and sure, now that he had his teeth in the idea. "This pack eats cats, but I'll stand by Fuzz. No dog will touch a hair on his back, if I can help it."

Fuzz leapt up from a hole in the floor — the window, Shep realized.

"Get out!" the cat hissed. His back was raised in an arch and his ears were flat against his head. His fangs were bared and his long, fluffy tail twitched like a snake ready to strike. "Shep-dog hurt Honey-friend with every bark!" The cat stepped forward, spitting with rage. "Fuzz not allow Shep-dog to hurt Honey-friend! Fuzz and Honey no need help from no-honor dog like Shep! Get out!"

Shep backed away from the cat, who was shivering with fury. Unsure what to woof, Shep left the two in the dark. If Honey wanted to punish him for his decision, that was her choice. She could be angry with him, but he felt good, finally having put that issue under paw. He could stand on that point at least — this pack eats cats. Done. No more worrying about that.

As Shep was hunting that afternoon, he met some of the other dogs from the pack, but he only recognized them because they nodded their snouts or wagged their tails at him. To Shep, they were all just dogs, strange dogs he'd never smelled before. He didn't like that the pack was so big that he didn't know each dog individually. *Next sun*, he thought, *I'm going to make a point to sniff out every dog in the den*. He wanted to know each one. What kind of leader could he be if he didn't know each dog, their particular strengths?

He rounded a corner into an alley and discovered Blaze dragging a struggling rat from beneath a slab of stone.

"Get out here, you filthy mound of fur!" she growled through her teeth.

Shep loped to her side. "Need another fang?"

Blaze ripped the rat out, and with a quick flick of her jaw, the rodent fell still. "No," she woofed, dropping it on the stone.

"I thought you hunted in a team," Shep barked, sniffing the rat. Lifeblood was a friendly scent to him now: the smell of a successful hunt. *No more nightmares for me*, he thought, happily.

"I did," Blaze snuffled. "But after our little fight, the other dogs think I'm cursed. Apparently, when you cross the Champion, you lose the privilege of having the others so much as sniff your tail."

"I'm sorry we had that fight," Shep woofed. "I know you believe you're right, but can't you smell that sometimes another dog might be on a good scent? Even if it's not the same scent you're tracking?"

"No," Blaze said, her bark soft, not defensive. "Not on something as important as this."

They padded down the alley in silence, panting in the

hot, humid afternoon air. The rat dangled from Blaze's jowls. The alley ended at a street. Blaze turned toward the boat, but Shep trotted in the other direction.

"You lost?" Blaze barked over her tail.

"I'm going to sniff around a little more," Shep woofed. "I hate to return home with empty jowls."

Blaze cocked her head, but then waved her tail and broke into a run down the street toward the boat. Shep trotted lazily in the dying light. The sky above him warmed to orange-blue, and the thin strips of cloud burned bright pink. It had felt good to hunt, good to be alone with the Outside, but it felt even better to be back with Callie and Blaze. And he would bark with Honey in the morning. Maybe she'd be less angry after sleeping on things for a night.

After that I'll woof with Oscar, he decided. *Maybe if I spend some time chewing a stick with the pup, he'll stop drooling all this Storm Shaker slobber.*

He was going to be the best teammate ever to walk on four paws. He rounded a corner to return to the boat, ready to get started on this whole leadership track again, and saw a snorty beast rooting in a bag of trash.

It wasn't one of Blaze's beasts — though it had horny, cloven paws, it was the size of Shep's crate, not a Car. It had a long, flat-nosed muzzle and largish ears on a fat head, with barely any neck separating it from the creature's thick shoulders. Bristles of hair trembled on its back, and a crooked tail hung from its muscled haunches.

The beast snorted and raised its snout from the refuse,

revealing bulky tusks that protruded from its thick jowls. Shep could run, leave this king among kibbles alone, or he could take the challenge that the Great Wolf had set before him.

Shep crouched and waited to smell how the beast would attack. He figured it would charge to take advantage of its tusks. He had to disable them as weapons. *Bite the ear.*

The beast squealed, then rushed at Shep, aiming to ram him in the chest. Shep held still, waited for the beast to get within range, then swung his body to the side and snapped onto the beast's ear. His fangs sunk into the leathery flesh and held.

The beast fought to free itself of Shep's bite, squealing like an old Car. It dragged Shep along the pavement and drove him into a wall. Shep managed to avoid getting smashed by hopping onto the beast's back for a heartbeat until it pulled away. The animal sank to the ground, then burst back to its paws and ran — anything to shake Shep's hold. But Shep's jaws were locked; he growled and tugged on the ear and knew it was only a matter of tiring the thing out.

After several more dives and dodges, the beast began to wheeze. The next time the creature sank to its belly, Shep jerked the ear, then released the flesh and pounded the beast in the chest with his paws. The thing was knocked off balance and crashed onto its side.

Shep had only a snoutful of heartbeats before it wriggled back onto its hoofs. He snapped his teeth around one thin ankle and broke the bone to make sure the beast couldn't regain its attack stance. Then he went for the neck. When he felt the monster's lifeblood pulse against his tongue, he knew he'd defeated it.

Shep stepped back from the body of his opponent, victorious and splattered with lifeblood. This beast had to be more than twice Shep's weight, and he'd defeated it. No dog had ever brought in such a kill. He was the master hunter! *Let Oscar tell a story about* this!

There was no way Shep was going to be able to drag the beast all the way back to the boat. Maybe he could get Blaze to help him? No, even with two dogs, it'd be too heavy. But he had to show her. She'd never believe him otherwise!

Shep scampered down the street back toward the den, jaws split in a grin and tongue lolling from his jaws. If he hurried, there would be just enough light left for a return trip.

CHAPTER 15
CRISIS AVERSION

Shep burst into the boat, panting heavily from running so hard back to the den. "Blaze!" he howled. "You won't believe what I did!"

Blaze stuck her muzzle out from the raised hall. She cocked her head, scenting how frazzled Shep was. "You smell like you just escaped a water lizard."

"Some flat-snouted beast," Shep managed between pants. "I killed it," he woofed. "It was huge, and all muscle, so you know it was powerful. But I beat it! You should have seen the battle."

Blaze's ears and tail perked up at the news. "Is it nearby? Can we bring it here?"

Shep licked his front paw. "No way," he woofed. "I told you, this thing was huge and solid as a rock."

Her tail dropped. "Well, that stinks."

Shep wagged his tail. "It's not far," he woofed. "I can show it to you before dark if we go now."

Blaze panted, her jowls curling into a smirk. "You think I'm upset because I can't see your trophy beast?" she grunted. "Sorry to slobber on your kibble, hero, but I was interested in your catch because I thought it might help with the minor crisis we have on our paws." Blaze then explained that all the kibble Shep had seen that afternoon — the pack's biggest catch ever — had disappeared.

"What happened?" he snuffled, shocked.

"Cats," Blaze snarled. "Cats have been stealing food out of the kibble room through a hole in the floor. They clawed the glass out of the broken window, so the food just poured down. They dug a tunnel under the boat to carry their stolen meal away. The felines got a bit greedy this time, and took almost the entire haul. By the time we got the smaller members of the defense team, the cats had escaped. Daisy and Waffle shoved pillows and cloth into the hole to plug it up. I was just about to go find you. We need a plan before the pack gets a whiff of what happened."

Shep chased around his brain for what to do. With each heartbeat, the news of the lost food was spreading. Shep heard the howling start up: "No food!" "Cats, measly cats broke our defenses?!" "Some dog was asleep at the watch!" "Does this mean no dinner? Again?"

Blaze's sharp cry ripped through the other voices. "It

wasn't our defense team!" she barked. "It was that traitor, Fuzz! He helped the cats infiltrate our den!"

Shep cocked his head at the girldog, dumbfounded. "Where'd you hear that?" he snuffled.

"Just follow my tail," Blaze replied in a low bark. "We can turn this to our advantage."

Some of the dogs nearby began to woof. "I *have* seen a cat slinking through the den." "Wasn't that cat with the dog who rescued me?" "He speaks dog, very strange."

"He's betrayed the pack!" howled Blaze. "We must throw the traitor out!"

Shep nipped Blaze on the scruff. "What are you barking? You know Fuzz had nothing to do with the theft."

"This will make the pack feel powerful, like they're in control," Blaze woofed. "If we can blame the cat, then we remain strong. Do you want to tell the pack that this boat has weak points? That we're vulnerable? We're on the verge of a riot here. How long until all the hungry, terrified, angry dogs in this cramped den start tearing into each other?"

Blaze turned her muzzle back to the crowd. "Sniff out the cat! Root out the traitor!"

"I can't let you do this," Shep yipped, his voice weak. He felt the floor slipping from beneath his paws. His heart raced; his lifeblood pounded so hard, he felt dizzy.

"It's done," Blaze snapped. She swung her snout and Shep saw the dogs pressing down the hall toward Honey's den, heard the howls of "Bring out the cat!"

Blaze looked him square in the snout. "Now's your chance," she barked. "You can take control of this stampede, or you can let it run right over you. But without you, this is the end of the pack."

Shep felt she was right. He had to do something. What was better — to let the pack tear itself apart just to save a cat, one lowly cat, or to stand strong and bring all the dogs together behind a cause? So the plan would result in the expulsion of a blameless cat, and most likely Honey would follow Fuzz, but they hated Shep and all the other dogs in the pack, anyway. Maybe this was a blessing. Honey and Fuzz would probably be happier on their own. Yeah. This was the right thing. In every way.

Shep stood tall and barked. "Bring the traitor to me!" he howled.

Fuzz, hissing and spitting and screaming a high-pitched screech that seemed not of this world, was carried in Mooch's jaws down the hall. He looked so small, ridiculously small, against Mooch's huge chest. Honey's cries rose up from the rear of the crowd.

"NO!" she wailed. "He's innocent! He's been with me! Stop! *Fuzz!*"

Shep's heart raced even faster. He felt the room spinning around him. Dogs were leaping on others' backs and barking and howling. It reminded Shep of the wild pack in the kibble den. The dogs were frenzied; the scent of rage and hunger and lifebloodlust swirled in the tight space.

Mooch spat the trembling Fuzz onto the floor in front of Shep. Fuzz lay flat on the metal and looked up at Shep with a hate that burned him like ice.

"Shep-dog know Fuzz not do this," Fuzz hissed. "Fuzz know you know."

Shep ignored the cat. Every muzzle in the room was on his scent. "I have seen this cat use the tunnels under the boat," Shep barked, stringing the woofs together from nothing. "He must have let the other cats in."

The pack seethed around him. The dogs' eyes were shot through with red lines, their tongues lolled, and their jowls dripped with slaver. Some of the dogs began to tussle with one another. Shep felt like he was losing control. One dog snapped at Fuzz's tail. Fuzz swiped at the dog with his paw. Honey shrieked from far away.

"Silence!" howled Oscar. The pup shoved his way to Shep's side and glared down at the trembling Fuzz. "This is yet another trial put to the Storm Shaker as a test of his valor by the Great Wolf. We, his packmates, have faced drought and hunger with him, have braved heat and vile beasts. Now, we face the betrayal of one of our own packmates. This cat has violated the sacred trust of the Great Wolf's Champion. The Storm Shaker took him in, offered him shelter, and he has turned against us all. The cat is the agent of the Black Dog! Let us throw him out to join his true master!"

A weird baying cry erupted from Oscar's followers; it

sounded like more than half the pack was in the club. The frenzied scent dissipated as Oscar's devotees lay down and began moaning Shep's name.

"What are you doing?" Shep grumbled.

"You want them to eat the cat?" snapped Oscar. "I figured Fuzz deserved better than that."

"I could have done something," Shep yipped, his bark weak and unconvincing.

"Why do you even care what happens with the pack?" growled Oscar. "You're never around the den. Go back to your hunting. We have the Storm Shaker. We don't need Shep anymore."

Oscar turned back to the crowd. "Mooch, you will bear the traitor to his exile!"

Mooch snatched up Fuzz in her jowls. The cat stopped struggling. He simply glared at Shep with his piercing green eyes, those strange glowing slits, until they disappeared in the crowd.

Honey burst through the pack of dogs, stopping only to spit slobber at Shep's paws. "You swore to protect him," she snarled. "Some Champion you've turned out to be." She shoved her way through the dogs, shrieking out Fuzz's name.

Blaze sat beside Shep as the majority of the dogs followed Mooch and Oscar toward the crushed floor to expel Fuzz from the boat. *At least they didn't eat him*, thought Shep. His stomach turned at the thought.

"Did that redirect the herd or what?" Blaze woofed. "Now you have a unified pack who will follow your barks." She tilted her head. "Aren't you going to thank me, hero? I made you the alpha."

Shep felt hollow inside. Blaze was right; the pack was unified. But it was a pack on the verge of turning wild. He could feel the Black Dog skulking in every shadow.

Blaze gave up waiting for a response. "We should organize the hunting teams," she barked. "We need to feed these dogs before they go absolutely squirrel-brained." She seemed in control and energized. Maybe Shep was wrong. Maybe the pack had only been excited. Maybe things weren't that far gone.

"Yeah," Shep yipped.

Blaze sighed. "Come on, big alpha Great Dog or whatever," she barked. "Pull your fur together! I'll get Virgil and meet you in the ceiling room."

Blaze leapt away from Shep into the main den. The heartbeat her scent left the air, Shep heard Callie's wheezy bark.

"Shep!" she moaned. "Get your fuzz head in here!"

Shep was confused — what did Callie have to be angry about? He loped down the hall to her dark sick den.

"Did I do something wrong?" he woofed.

Callie stared at him, brown eyes bulging from their sockets. "Wrong? You have to ask me if you did something wrong?"

"What, throwing out Fuzz? You never wanted him here in the first place."

Callie lifted herself onto her paws. "Whether I wanted him at first doesn't change the fact that he was part of the pack before you and that snarling mob tossed him out on his tail."

"He could have been helping those cats," Shep woofed. "I did see him under the boat."

"For the love of treats, listen to yourself!" Callie broke into a fit of coughing. "You threw the cat out — *cough cough* — for no reason other than to make yourself feel powerful!"

"No," Shep snarled, "to make the *pack* feel powerful. How would it have gone over to tell every dog that our defense team couldn't defend them from a couple of scavenging cats?"

Callie stumbled toward him. "Oh, so whenever the pack needs to feel powerful, we won't tell them that we need to increase our defenses? *Cough!* No, we'll just blame some totally innocent and defenseless dog, someone no one likes, anyway. We'll blame Rufus! Perfect, Shep! Next time you need to increase morale, nose out the nasty old squaredog."

"Callie, you're going too far —"

"Even better — *cough!* — let's drive out all the newborn pups! They're eating kibble without offering any help hunting. And the dams, too! And all the old dogs who can't do anything! All the yappers, Shep! Let's kick them all out!" Callie was panting hard, her bark a screech. Her whole body trembled.

Her back legs gave out, and her rump dropped onto the

floor. She let her chest slide down onto the metal and rested her head on her paws.

"I would never let the pack attack another dog." Shep laid his head down beside Callie's.

Callie moved her muzzle to the other side of her paws. "Several suns ago, I recall you swearing to defend that cat you just allowed to be hauled out of his den."

"The pack was feeling vulnerable —"

"Save your excuses, Shep. Just leave me alone." Callie shuffled on her paws so that she faced the back wall of the den, away from Shep.

Shep crept out of the room and found Blaze waiting with Virgil.

"Cat's gone," she woofed. "Honey went with him. The pack's settling down in the main den. The defense team is watching from the edges to take care of any random fights that might break out. I told Oscar to tell one of his stories to keep them occupied."

Blaze began dictating a hunting plan. She wanted to track the cats through the hole, kill them, and take back all the kibble.

Shep agreed to whatever she said. He felt like his heart had beat all the lifeblood out of him, as if his body was full of stuffing, like a toy's. As soon as they were dismissed, he used the back staircase-hole to leave the boat without passing through the main den. The last thing he wanted to hear was Oscar weaving his lies.

He found Dover out by his overturned boat, pacing circles in the dirt. The old dog smelled upset.

"I saw the pack chase out the cat," he woofed. "What was that about?"

Shep explained about the kibble, about how he needed to keep the pack together. "I could feel their anxiety when they heard cats had stolen the meal. Every dog's so hungry, I think the loss of food was like the flea that sent the dog tearing out its own fur." Shep lay down. "Blaze had the idea of blaming Fuzz, and it worked."

Dover remained standing. "Don't you blame Blaze for this madness." His bark was flat.

Shep stood, shocked by the unfriendly tone. "I'm not blaming her," he woofed. "It *was* her idea."

"And you followed her track?" Dover grumbled. "Tell me, pup, if it was just you, would you have thrown the cat out?"

Shep scented where this was going. "It wasn't *just* me, Dover," he barked. "I had the whole pack breathing down my tail. What was I supposed to do? Let them go wild and tear one another apart?"

"I guess it depends on what kind of pack you're running," Dover woofed. "Do you want to lead a pack that throws out its weakest members to make itself feel strong?"

Shep sat and scratched his shoulder. "Now you sound like Callie."

Dover sat beside him. "Well, whose scent smells right: Callie's or Blaze's?"

Shep let the woofs hang there, like flies in the darkening evening. He didn't need to answer; he felt it in his gut. Callie was right. It had been wrong to throw out Fuzz. Better to let the pack fall apart than to lead a wild pack. They were loping down that track, Shep knew. How long until they were completely wild? How long until he was the Black Dog, watching his underlings tearing the fur from their backs?

CHAPTER 16
THE CHAMPION SHRUGS

Shep loped back into the den and nearly bumped snouts with Blaze. She was the last dog Shep wanted to smell at that heartbeat. He lowered his tail.

"Where've you been?" Blaze woofed, either ignoring or not noticing Shep's reaction.

"We were wrong," Shep woofed. "We shouldn't have blamed Fuzz."

Blaze gave a quick sigh, flicking her ears. "Wrong or no, it's done," she barked. "What is it with you, Shep? Every time you make a decision, you end up backing away from it. Do you want to lead this pack or not?" She looked him hard in the muzzle.

"No, Blaze," Shep woofed. "I don't want to lead *this* pack.

This pack is going wild. We need to try to bring some order back to things, reorganize the teams —"

Blaze cut his bark short. "Enough," she snapped. "You really think this is the time to paw around with your posture? The pack is like a herd of beasts on the edge of stampede — you show the slightest waver in your stance, and they'll crush you. Why do I have to keep explaining this?"

Shep straightened his stance, raising his head and tail. "You're wrong, Blaze," he barked. "Strength doesn't come from attacking the weakest members, or from scaring dogs into thinking you come from the Great Wolf. Strength comes from doing what you know from your claws to your nose is the right thing. And it was wrong to blame Fuzz for something we know he didn't do."

"A real leader does whatever he has to do to keep every dog alive," Blaze snarled. "If you're not willing to put your fur on the line for these dogs, then I will." She bounded away from him into the main part of the den.

Shep wondered if he should follow her, stop her from doing whatever she was about to do, but he didn't want to fight with her anymore. It seemed all he and his friends did was fight. He snuck through the back staircase-hole down to the bottom floor and found Callie lying in the dark. Her breathing was even, but Shep could smell that she was awake.

"I came back to apologize," Shep woofed.

"You don't owe *me* an apology," Callie barked.

"Then what can I do?" Shep crouched down and crept closer to Callie's back.

Callie raised her head, then shifted around so that she lay facing Shep. "For starters, you can find Honey and Fuzz and make sure they're okay."

"I will," Shep woofed, relief flooding through him at the kindness in Callie's barks.

"And then you have to get rid of Blaze."

Shep pulled his muzzle back as if slapped. "What? Why?" he yipped.

"She's tearing this pack apart," Callie woofed. "If you fight her and drive her away, the dogs will smell that you're still in charge. With the help of Oscar's club, we can bring the pack together again."

Shep stood and sat back, away from Callie. Nothing in her barks felt right. "No, Oscar's club is as bad as Blaze's ideas about being the alpha."

"But you can use Oscar's group," Callie woofed, stepping closer to him. "The pup loves you, and only wants to please you. If you give him a kibble of positive attention, I think we can sway his stories however we need to. In fact, I've been coming up with a new legend we can tell in the morning —"

"Absolutely not!" Shep barked. "Callie, that club is nothing but lies. I don't want dogs to follow me because they think I'm something I'm not. I want them to follow me because they believe I'll do what's right."

"I keep telling you, it's not about you anymore! We have to do what's right for the pack!"

"I won't do that, Callie," Shep snuffled. "Not even for you." He padded out of the room.

Callie's barks followed him down the hall. "They won't follow just any dog, Shep! They need to believe you're more than they are! They're just pets, scared pets!"

Shep escaped as fast as his paws could carry him from the room. Then he had an idea. He had to stop the pack from tumbling out of control. He felt like he was fighting the storm all over again — huge things swirled around him, threatening to tear everything he cared about away from him. But this time, he could do something. He could tear the storm apart before it had the chance to do the same to him.

Shep sniffed out Oscar, who was woofing quietly with Odie and another dog Shep didn't know.

"Oscar," he barked.

The pup looked over his tail at Shep. "One heartbeat, Champion," he yipped. "We have to finish planning tomorrow's story of your greatness."

Shep grabbed Oscar by the scruff and lifted him off the floor. "Now, pup," Shep growled through his teeth.

Oscar snarled and squirmed in Shep's jaws. "Put me down! I'm not a weakling anymore! I'll have my followers get you for this!"

"You think your followers would attack the mighty Champion of the Great Wolf?"

Shep dragged the pup out of the boat and plopped him down on a patch of grass beneath a tree. The palm had been stripped bare by the winds. Now, its fronds were brown whips that clattered like twigs in the breeze.

Oscar shook his fur and sat, anger seething off him in waves. "You have my undivided attention," he snarled. "What's so important?"

"You're disbanding the club tonight," Shep barked, not loudly, but with a tone that suggested the issue was not open for discussion.

"Disbanding?" Oscar yipped. "Why?"

"I never wanted to be smelled the way you've gotten these dogs to smell me," Shep woofed.

"You like my stories when they help you, like with Blaze and saving the cat," Oscar growled. "You like my group when it gives you power, but if I don't do exactly as you say, you want to end it?" The pup set his little jaw and squinted his deep brown eyes.

"That's not why I want you to disband it," Shep woofed.

"Are you afraid I'll start running the pack?" Oscar snapped, standing. "You're just jealous! I can't believe it! Well, you're right to have your tail between your legs. Where would you be right now without my club? I'll tell you: You'd be alone in this den with no one but Callie to sniff your tail."

Shep's jaws hung open like a trap. Had the pup just actually asserted dominance? Shep shook his muzzle. No. Not Oscar. But he did bare his fangs. Or did he? No. He couldn't have. He wouldn't have.

Shep shook himself and lowered his head, taking a more friendly stance. "Why are you so angry, Oscar?" he woofed softly. "Let's woof about things and maybe you'll start to smell what I'm smelling."

"Oh, yeah?" snarled Oscar. "What do you smell?"

"I smell a pup who's let a little submission from some older dogs turn his nose onto the wrong scent," Shep said in his most gentle bark.

The pup reset his jaw. "I knew it," he growled. "You *are* jealous. Well, you can take your commands and bark them right up this palm tree. I gave you a chance to be a part of the club and you kicked dirt in my snout, so forget it. I'm not disbanding my club, not ever!"

Shep glared down at the pup, who growled back at him, fangs bared. Who was this dog? Where was the sweet pup who would have given his claws to curl next to Shep's snout? *What did I do to him?*

There was a chance of barking with the old Oscar, but the pup was now sick with hate. Shep was sure he deserved some portion of that anger, but it wasn't just about him anymore — he had to save the pack from itself. Shep sighed. "You leave me no choice."

He bayed as loudly as he could, a piercing cry that echoed off all the buildings surrounding the plaza. The dogs inside the den pressed their paws against the glass. They began trickling out onto the dark street, and soon they surrounded Shep and the pup. Some dogs chattered their teeth nervously; others whimpered, asking why Oscar was there, why Shep had howled them out.

"I called you together to clear up a few things," Shep

barked. "I want you to know that the stories that Oscar and his friends have been telling you are lies."

"Are not!" screeched the pup.

Shep lifted his great paw and placed it on Oscar's head, then smushed him gently into the grass. The pup wriggled and whined to get free, but Shep held him.

Shep continued, "I am not the Great Wolf, nor his Champion. I'm not special in any way. I'm just a dog who wants to help other dogs, any animal in need. I'm a pretty great hunter, and a well-trained fighter. And I'm willing to fight for you, but not alone. I work with Higgins and Callie and Virgil and Blaze because they help me to help you. If any dog doesn't like that fact, they're free to leave the pack."

He stood proud, staring into the eyes of the nearest dogs. Some seemed calmed by his words; some tails began to wag. Blaze stood near the edge of the crowd. Her head was cocked and she waved her tail.

Shep lifted his paw off Oscar. The pup fell away from Shep, gasping and hacking. He glared up at Shep with a hatred that sent shivers through Shep's fur.

"How could you?" Oscar growled. The pup looked at the faces of the nearest dogs, and they looked down at him with something Shep could only describe as pity. Oscar turned his muzzle back to Shep. "You'll regret this," he snapped. "Without me, this pack will fall apart. And you know it." The pup scampered away into the night.

The dogs began crawling back into the boat. Blaze came to Shep's side.

"So you do want to lead," she woofed. "Then I won't stand in your way."

"I'm not leading the way you want me to lead," Shep said.

"It may not be exactly how I thought of leadership," Blaze woofed. "But it works for this mess of pets."

Shep started to lope away from her.

"Where are you going?" Blaze barked. "We have to get these dogs some food."

"Have some dogs drag back that beast I killed," Shep replied over his tail. "I have to find Honey and Fuzz."

"Are you squirrel-brained?" Blaze cried. "You don't even know where they went. The pack needs you!"

"I have to make things right," Shep woofed. "I can't leave them alone in this wild place."

"You can't leave your pack!" Blaze yelped. "Shep!"

Her barks reverberated behind him, but Shep kept running. He sniffed each passing tree, piece of rubble, and wall for some scent of Honey and the cat. Once they were back in the pack, everything would be fixed. He was finally on the right scent and things were coming together.

CHAPTER 17
THE BLACK DOG RISES

The sky was a dull, metallic gray and a light drizzle had begun to fall. Shep had roamed in circles all night and all the next sun, desperate to find a trace of Honey's scent, but he'd had no luck. He'd catch a whiff of her on a scrap of tree bark, but the trail would lead nowhere, or would fade into nothing. The closest he'd gotten was here, on a dock floating in the canal — an old scent, but one suggesting Honey had been foolish enough to cross the canal alone. Why would she do such a thing? Wild dogs? Shep lifted his snout at the thought. *No, Great Wolf, please.* Had they found her?

Shep sniffed the water — no scent but the slime of chemicals on the surface. A tree was jammed into the wall of the canal not far from where he stood. Shep padded over to the edge of the dock, then hopped onto the tree. It gave under Shep's weight and he wavered on his paws, but regained his balance. The surface of the water was pocked by the drizzle and the only sound was the soft plash of rain.

He crept along the tree trunk, out into the canal. The rain-dimpled surface made it hard to watch for any water lizards below, but hopefully it also hid him and any ripples he sent across the water from them. The end of the tree trunk was a full stretch from the opposite canal wall, and the dock was another stretch away from the tree along the stone slab.

It felt good to be faced with a problem of strength — something Shep was good at. He tensed his leg muscles and bounced lightly, gauging the spring of the tree. With an explosion from his hind legs, he burst into the air. He stretched his forelegs and neck, reaching for the dock. His front claws scratched the metal surface, but his hind legs fell short and crashed into the fetid water.

Shep struggled to pull himself up onto the slippery dock, then he felt it — something large and rough rubbed along his submerged rear paw. He clawed at the metal. *Come on!* He gnashed his teeth as he strained to haul his rump out of the canal. Finally, he hooked a back claw onto the edge of the dock and thrust his hindquarters onto the platform. Just as he did, a knobby green-gray snout rose from the dark depths of the water, eyes glinting atop it like fat droplets. Shep backed away from the water. The great beast opened its jagged-toothed maw and hissed sour breath, then closed its mouth and sank into the black.

Shep panted, mesmerized by the appearance of the strange monster. What had it been trying to say? A chill shivered along Shep's fur. Was that the thing that had eaten Cheese? Had it taken Honey, too?

Shep sniffed around the edge of the dock. A flight of stairs ran from it up to the street. No, Honey had survived the crossing. Shep smelled both her scent and Fuzz's on the stone. *At least she made it this far.* But Shep smelled other dogs' smells, some from around the same heartbeat as when Honey had passed. She'd been running — but from whom?

The trail was easy to follow on this side of the canal. Honey had been careless, knocking into boxes and bins as she ran. The sun was fully in the sky when Shep found the alley where Honey lay on a flattened pile of thick, brown box-paper. Lifeblood dyed the paper surrounding her body a deep red-brown. Shep raced to her side and sniffed her muzzle. Her breath was weak, barely ruffling his whiskers, but she was alive. *Thank the Great Wolf!*

"Honey," Shep whimpered. "I'm here to save you. I can bring you back to the den. Boji can help you."

Honey's eyelids fluttered. "Fuzz," she groaned.

"No, it's Shep," he woofed. He glanced around the alley — he neither smelled nor saw a trace of the cat. "Can you walk?"

Honey lifted her head a paw's length off the ground. "You

found me," she moaned. "He said you'd come for me, but I didn't believe him."

Shep cocked his head. "Who said I'd come for you?"

"He said his name was Zeus."

It was like the street tilted. Everything slid in Shep's mind, falling into some black crevice. Out of the blackness rose Zeus's muzzle as it was pulled away from him by the wave, the face of his best friend, the dog who tried to kill him.

He survived.

Honey coughed and lifeblood-stained spittle spattered the box-paper.

"Zeus did this to you?" Shep yipped, trying to keep his voice from shaking.

Honey gave a feeble wave of her tail.

Emotions roiled inside Shep like a storm — joy at his friend's survival; horror at the thought of his return, of having to fight him again; rage at what he'd done to Honey. The feelings threatened to tear Shep to shreds.

"He left me alive to give you a message," Honey moaned, wincing at the expulsion of her own breath. "He said that he wanted revenge." Her head fell back onto the paper. "I don't know why hurting me would give him revenge."

Shep lay down beside Honey and licked her muzzle. "Hurting you was his way of hurting me," he woofed quietly. "I'm so sorry, Honey. I should never have let the pack throw Fuzz out."

Honey's breathing was a mere trickle of air through her nostrils. Her eyes struggled to remain open, then she gave up and let them close. "Find Fuzz," she wheezed. "Protect him."

"I will," Shep whimpered. "I swear I will."

Her breath slowed. Each exhalation sounded like the cat's name; Shep wasn't sure whether it was an incantation or a reminder. Shep licked her jowls and whimpered sorry over and over to her. He lay beside her until she was at rest. Then he pulled a piece of box-paper over her and wished her a quick journey to the Great Wolf.

"What Shep-dog do to Honey-friend?" Fuzz screeched from the roof above. The cat sprang down onto a pile of rubble, approaching Shep with ears back, tail up and twitching, and hackles raised.

"I came to bring you both back," Shep woofed, lying down to show Fuzz he meant no harm. "But her injuries were too bad."

"Where Honey-friend?" The cat loped past Shep to the box pile, where Honey's tail peeked from beneath a shadow. Fuzz squirmed under the paper and let loose a terrible cry. "Honey-friend!"

Shep buried his snout in his paws, not wanting to disturb the poor feline. Fuzz sounded about as miserable as any animal could get.

After several heartbeats, Fuzz crawled out from under the box-paper. "Fuzz spend many cycle trying to care for Honey-friend." He sat near Shep, then folded his body down into a compact knot. "Fuzz care for Honey-friend since she is baby-dog. But Fuzz fail. Big dog attack, and Fuzz hide like insect. Fuzz not worth the fur in a hairball." The cat's eyes were closed. He held himself still, as if even the slightest twitch of his whiskers would break him apart.

"You couldn't have fought off this dog, Fuzz, not even with four clawed paws and all the desire in your heart." Shep crept closer to the cat and dared a quick lick of friendship. "If this is any dog's fault, it's mine."

The cat remained still as stone.

"Honey was thinking of you in her last breath," Shep woofed. "She made me promise to protect you."

"Shep-dog's protection." Hate dripped from his words. "That what got Fuzz and Honey-friend shut out in first place," Fuzz hissed.

"I was a bad dog," Shep woofed. "I let you and Honey down. But I'm trying to do the right thing." He crept closer to Fuzz, so that his nose was next to the cat's face. "Please, Fuzz. I swear that I will protect you with all the power in my jaws."

The cat opened his eyes, their color an eerie yellow-green in the gray light. "Fuzz go," he spat. "But only because Honey-friend wish it."

Shep rolled slightly and wagged his tail, offering Fuzz his usual shoulder-perch, but the cat unwrapped himself, then stretched, arching his back in the most unnatural fashion.

"Fuzz prefer walk."

* * *

As they neared the boat, the smell of spilled lifeblood baking in the sun washed over Shep like the wave. Shep broke into a run and Fuzz scrambled to keep up beside him. The first body was on the street before the plaza — a small dog, not one Shep knew, but a pet. He could tell by the collar still around the dog's neck.

So this is what Zeus meant by revenge.

The boat lay on its side as always, but bits of the den inside were strewn about the street in front of it. Stuffing and feathers torn from pillows formed white clouds on the pavement. The bodies of dead dogs — mostly pets — had been dragged into piles near the unused small boats, some of which had been shoved out of place or smashed to pieces. The survivors huddled in groups Outside the den, whimpering softly. Upon smelling Shep, they growled.

Inside was worse. The den reeked of lifeblood. Hurt dogs moaned from every corner. Shep raced to Callie's sick den — *Please let her be all right!* He didn't know who he was asking, since the Great Wolf had apparently abandoned him and his friends to the ferocious anger of the Black Dog.

He found Callie in her room, alive, barking with Blaze and some of the defense team. They scented him before he could so much as woof hello.

"Glad you came back," Callie snapped.

Shep dug for words. "What happened?"

Blaze growled, then barked, "Appears your old pal Zeus is alive and a little angry with you. He thinks attacking some helpless pets is going to settle things." She didn't even look at him.

"But Zeus attacked Honey," Shep woofed, trying to piece together the events of the last sun. "I found her." He flicked his snout at Fuzz, who was huddled in the corner. "Zeus killed Honey to get back at me."

Blaze lowered her muzzle and glared at Shep over her shoulder. "I guess killing Honey wasn't enough to get the point across."

"I didn't know," Shep woofed. "How could I? If I'd known —"

"What?" Blaze snarled. "If you'd known your friend and his pack of wild dogs were coming to massacre us, you'd have listened to me and helped plan our defenses instead of running out for nearly two suns to find one stupid girldog and her cat?"

Shep felt the world sliding again, everything crumbling beneath his paws. He'd done the right thing. He'd had to save Honey — how was he to know she'd already be as good as dead when he found her? He'd done the right thing! Why was he being punished?

"Virgil's dead," Blaze continued, her bark flat and cold as a blade. "I led the defense team after he fell."

"I didn't know," Shep whimpered. He crouched low to the floor for security. "I didn't know."

"We're ending the war this sun," Blaze snapped. "I'm leading the remaining defense team on an assault of the wild dogs' lair."

"No," Shep woofed. "Don't go — Wait, how do we know where their lair is?"

Daisy stepped out of the shadows dragging Oscar by the scruff. "Ask the pup," she growled.

Oscar looked like a wilted leaf: Every part of him sagged. When Daisy dropped him onto the floor, he just lay there like a puddle.

"Oh, no, Oscar," Shep yelped. "What did you do?"

"I was angry," the pup yipped. "You said those things and made me look like a weasel in front of every dog. I sniffed out the wild pack. Zeus took me in." The pup lifted his muzzle, his eyes wide and watery. "I didn't know, Shep! You have to believe me! I didn't know what he was going to do!"

"What did you think he would do?" Blaze growled. "Drop by to share some kibble?"

The pup cringed, becoming an even smaller and more pathetic pile of fur. "I didn't know," he whimpered.

"You didn't think," snapped Callie. "Neither of you. And now we've lost some of our best fight dogs. Bernie's injured a paw, and Hulk's got a nasty gash on his face."

"They'll be fine," Blaze barked. "I've already discussed an attack strategy with them."

"Attack strategy?" woofed Shep, trying to keep up. "Why are we attacking them? Shouldn't we regroup here? Rebuild our defenses?"

"I hate to tell you," Blaze barked, standing, "but we had a vote while you were out and I've been chosen to lead the pack. Seems the dogs have lost their faith in Shep the Great Woof."

"Wolf," Shep corrected.

"Whatever," Blaze snapped.

"Don't do it," Shep grunted. "I know you don't care what I think, but I know Zeus. He'll expect a counterattack."

"He won't expect this counterattack," Blaze said, pride oozing from her barks. "I've modified my herding commands. We're going to flank them, drive them into an alley, and end this war."

"Zeus is the best fight dog I've ever battled with," Shep woofed, quietly. "He'd take you all out, even if your plan worked."

"Don't be so sure," Blaze growled.

"I am sure," Shep replied. "Don't go, Blaze."

"So I should listen to the dog who abandoned his friends the very heartbeat they needed him?" Blaze shoved her chest out and growled right in Shep's muzzle. "I guess I listen about as well as you."

She shoved past him and out into the hall. She let off a screaming howl that rattled the walls of the den, then bounded out to begin her war.

Shep closed his eyes. He'd failed them all, every dog in his pack. Why *should* Blaze listen to him? What wisdom, in all these suns, had he really shown?

"We should get all the dogs back into the boat," Callie woofed. "In case you're right." She stood and her little legs trembled under her. She stepped tentatively, as if afraid the floor might suck her under. Shep lowered his muzzle and rested it against her shoulder, holding her up.

"It was terrible," Callie whimpered in his ear. "Zeus's howl rang through the den like thunder. He's as angry as the storm, Shep, and he seems set on tearing your world apart."

"Did he come after you?" Shep whimpered.

"I hid under the boat, where the cats had invaded." Callie looked at Daisy, who lowered her muzzle. "Higgins hid as many of us small dogs as he could, piled the food on top of us to hide our scent." Her barks caught in her throat. "The stupid furface even tried to fight him."

Shep felt his back legs give out and he slumped to the floor. Virgil killed, and Higgins, too — his closest friends, gone. Zeus's fury knew no limits. Every dog who'd so much as wagged a tail at Shep was going to be punished.

Shep set his jaw. *No more.* He placed his paws beneath his body and rose like a thundercloud. "No more," he growled. He raised his muzzle and bayed at the ceiling, "NO MORE!" He felt strength run through him like lightning. He would defend this den until the last drop of lifeblood pulsed from his heart. He would make this right. He would protect these dogs. He would not fail them again.

"Get all the small dogs," Shep barked to Daisy. "Hide them under the boat."

"What about Oscar?" she woofed. The pup still cringed at her paws.

"I don't think he's going anywhere," Shep barked. Daisy

sniffed the pup, then wagged her knot-tail and bounded into the hall.

Shep lowered his snout so he was growling directly into Oscar's ear. "You want the pack to forgive you?" he growled.

The pup shivered and yelped in reply.

"Then you dig out that tunnel we filled to prevent the cats from stealing our food." Shep nosed the pup. "You stay there, and if trouble strikes, you lead the dogs out that tunnel to safety."

The pup raised his head. "Lead them?"

Shep looked the pup in his eyes: They were huge brown pools rimmed in black, expressing an endless misery.

"You can do it," Shep yipped. He licked Oscar's head.

The pup whimpered, cringing. Then placed his paws under him. "I'll do it," he woofed.

Oscar scampered out of the den, shrinking away from Callie as he passed her.

"That's your plan?" Callie woofed. She lowered her rump and scratched her ear. "We hide under the boat and hope the wild dogs think we've moved on?"

"No," Shep barked. "You hide under the boat and I give Zeus what he came for."

CHAPTER 18
THE PLAN

Shep organized his defense of the den. He knew that Zeus would expect a retaliatory attack — it was what Shep would expect an opponent to do. Zeus would therefore avoid whatever lair his wild pack had been using. He would most likely attack the boat again, in hopes of finding Shep returned from scenting out Honey. Even if Shep was wrong, he thought it better to be prepared than caught unawares.

Most of the bigger dogs had left with Blaze to attack the wild pack's den. Boji stayed behind to help care for the injured dogs from the first wave of attack, and Dover had declined Blaze's offer.

"I thought you might need another set of claws," Dover woofed to Shep.

Shep left Boji to tend the injured and had Dover sniff over the whole of the den to identify any points of weakness.

"I need to know where the wild dogs can get in," he instructed. "I don't want them sneaking up on me from behind."

Fuzz, who'd been hanging in the shadows near Shep, boring into his fur with those grass green eyes, stepped forward. "Fuzz help," the cat barked. "Help Shep-dog sniff out any secret holes. Help protect dog-pack."

"You don't have to, Fuzz," Shep woofed. "You can stay with Callie."

"Shep-dog finally act with honor," Fuzz meowed. "Fuzz always help dog who act with honor."

"You're a good friend," Shep said, tail wagging.

"Fuzz say nothing about friend," he hissed, then meowed a short laugh and flicked his tail.

"Okay," Shep yipped. "I won't beg for more than you're offering."

Shep left Dover and Fuzz to scour the den for weaknesses, and began sniffing out the dogs who moped Outside. He dragged any that couldn't or wouldn't walk with him by the scruff back into the boat. Scenting Ginny and Rufus crouched under an overturned cold box, Shep stuck his snout under to bark at them and got a claw in the nose.

"Away, you rapscallion!" Ginny cried.

"Ginny, it's Shep!" Shep licked his nose where she'd scratched the skin.

"Shep?" A narrow white snout appeared from beneath the thick wall of the cold box. The shiny black nose sniffed. "By Lassie's golden fur, it *is* Shep!"

The poofy girldog wriggled her way out from under the cold box. "Oh, Shep, you wouldn't believe the mess that poor, misguided pup got us into."

"Weren't you the dog who was guiding him these last suns?" Shep asked, cocking his head.

Ginny stiffened and her tail drooped. "Well, he went and led those wild dogs right to us. I never told him to do that."

Shep licked Ginny's head. "Oscar's tearing his own fur out over what happened."

"Well, he should!" yapped Rufus as he squirmed out of his hiding place. "I nearly lost my tail tuft to one of those mongrels!"

"Every dog makes mistakes," Shep woofed. "Some lash out at their friends in anger, like Oscar. Some are afraid to make hard choices, like me. Some steal kibble when they know every dog is starving."

The squaredog lowered his snout. "Yes, well," he grumbled.

"Now's the time when we need to stick together," Shep woofed. "Can I trust you to sniff out any pack members that are hiding? We need to get them all inside the den."

"Inside the den?" Rufus cried. "We'll be shredded to kibble in heartbeats trapped in there!"

Shep nipped Rufus on the scruff. "Don't let fear keep you from being a part of the pack," he woofed. "I have a plan."

Shep returned to the boat and scented out Dover and Fuzz.

"The den's as safe as it ever was," Dover woofed. "There are the two ways in on the crushed floor, then the door in the rear window-wall in the main den, which was busted open and is now just an empty frame. Also the holes on the bottom floor under the boat, but the wild dogs won't use them."

"Fuzz check in walls," the cat meow-barked. "All safe. Found one bug. Bug eaten."

"Should we start setting up defenses inside the boat?" barked Dover. "Like we did in the kibble den?"

"If my plan works," woofed Shep, "we won't have to worry about the wild dogs getting into the den."

Dover sat and scratched an itch on his neck. "If it's not too much of a bother," he snuffled, "might I ask what exactly your plan is?"

"I'd tell you," Shep yipped, grinning, "but you'd only say I'm crazy."

"Can Fuzz help?" meowed Fuzz, waving his tail.

"Not with this," Shep replied. "But you can help Ginny and Rufus collect any stragglers. Remember, every dog has to be inside the den."

The sun was beginning to fall in the sky. Shep figured Zeus would attack again near sunset, though he couldn't be sure of anything. He had to set his plan in motion now, whether Zeus was there or not.

Shep bounded down the streets back toward where he'd crossed the canal to find Honey. He loped down the steps to the dock, leapt onto the tree trunk, which was still jammed into the wall, then began hopping up and down. Small ripples shimmered across the canal, becoming larger and larger waves.

Come on, come on . . .

Shep then sprang from the tree into the water. He spread his legs out to produce the largest splash possible, then paddled madly for the dock.

You've got to be hungry . . . a big thing like you . . .

Just as he pulled himself fully onto the dock he saw it: two bulbous eyes glittering, a ridged snout sliding through the water.

"Come and get me!" Shep barked, then scrambled up the steps.

The water lizard floated still as a stick.

Shep jumped back down onto the dock. "What, I'm not tasty enough for you?"

Maybe he didn't smell tasty enough. Shep took a deep breath, then bit his own tongue. Lifeblood gushed into his mouth. He spat slobber laced with the stuff onto the beast's snout.

"Like that?" he barked.

The monster's eyes flashed. Shep smelled an eerie scent — the water lizard was excited.

Shep spat again, this time on the dock.

The lizard lifted its snout out of the water and smashed it down onto the platform. Shep was thrown from his paws and landed on his side. The dock angled down toward the water, where the lizard floated with its long, tooth-lined mouth open wide. Its tongue slithered in its jaws.

Shep began to slide toward the beast.

"Oh, no, you don't!" he howled. He slammed a hind paw against the monster's bottom jawbone, giving himself the pawhold he needed. He flipped himself over and clawed his way back up the dock.

The water lizard hissed, then began climbing after him.

It's working!

Shep sprang off the dock onto the stone of the canal wall and bounded up the steps. The water lizard struggled to pull himself onto the dock. The platform rocked with the effort of the gigantic beast, but the lizard managed to drag itself entirely out of the water.

For a heartbeat, the madness of Shep's plan shocked him to stillness. The water lizard was three stretches long at least, with jaws longer than Shep's forelegs. Shep had woken something worse than his worst nightmare and then spat on it. *Callie's going to chew my ear off for this one.*

Shep bolted up the steps, barking at the water lizard the whole way. The beast was surprisingly nimble on land, and was quickly hoisting its vast bulk up the steps after Shep.

At the top, Shep took off at his fastest pace, and even then, the water lizard nipped at his tail. The thing raced behind him, its flipper-paws slapping the stone like shoes. Shep's heart was in his throat, his paws burned on the hot pavement, but he pressed on, faster and faster.

He neared the boat, his tongue lolling from his mouth, foamy spittle lining his jowls, and scented the wild dogs.

Right on time . . .

CHAPTER 19
THE LAST BATTLE

Shep pushed his legs even harder, giving every last drop of energy to his speed. He burst like a Car onto the open plaza surrounding the boat.

Zeus stood on top of the boat, a silhouette against the fiery clouds. Beneath him crowded a mass of wild dogs, yipping and snapping and jumping on one another's backs.

"Zeus!" Shep screamed, his bark strained.

The horned shadow of Zeus's head turned. "The King of the Yappers returns!"

The entire pack of wild dogs launched toward Shep, and he sprinted straight into that mass of muzzles. When he could see the whites of the nearest dog's eyes, he turned and sprang onto a pile of wreckage.

The wild pack had a heartbeat to react, but most had no idea what to make of the gigantic lizard lumbering toward them. Then the beast opened its jaws. The wild dogs understood.

With a chorus of shrieks, the wild pack exploded like bees from a hive. The lizard tore into the fur of the nearest dogs and lifeblood rained down onto the stone. Fear swept over the dogs like a sickness. They scrambled into buildings and down alleys, whimpering and crying like beaten pups, anything to get away from the horrible monster.

Shep looked up from the mayhem of dogs and lizard. Zeus remained on the boat. Shep skirted the edge of the buildings and ducked into the crushed floor. He clambered up the steering counter, then pulled himself through the tangled beams of the ceiling. Just as he emerged onto the windows over the main den, Zeus tackled him.

"Thought you'd gotten rid of me?" Zeus snarled.

Up close, Shep saw that his friend was striped with scars along his muzzle and flank. "Fought your way to the top, did you?" Shep barked.

"Worried your way to the bottom, I hear," Zeus snapped. He lunged at Shep, catching the edge of his scruff.

Shep dove onto his shoulder, then hit Zeus in the chest with his forepaws, throwing the boxer onto the slick surface of the windows.

Zeus sprang to his paws. "It's all about decisions, Shep," he snarled. "I'm not afraid to make the hard choices."

"Like the decision to betray your friend?" Shep growled.

Zeus howled and jumped at Shep's head, fangs slashing. Shep feinted high, then rolled, scraping his claws along Zeus's exposed underbelly. Zeus cried out and fell against the windows, then hopped to his paws.

A strange roar rose up from the street. The wild dogs ran in circles, some bolting for cover, others attacking the lizard with little success. The monster seemed to be calling for something.

The monster cried again, its bizarre voice ringing around the walls enclosing it. Shep saw something disturb the debris floating in the canal near the bottom of the ramp. Two more water lizards slithered out of the deep, trailing ribbons of weed and refuse from their spiked hides. A smile crawled across Shep's jowls. *I command a whole* pack *of monsters!*

Shep swiped at Zeus with his fangs, catching him unawares while he was staring at the advancing lizards. Zeus yelped and stumbled back. Shep ran for the crushed floor, hoping to jump down and better direct his scaly soldiers. As he was about to drop down the rear wall, he felt fangs catch his hind paw.

"Not just yet, friend," Zeus growled. He pulled back, dragging Shep across the windows. Broken glass cut his skin.

On Zeus's next tug, Shep slammed his other hind leg into Zeus's snout, forcing him to drop the paw. Shep swung his head around, flinging his rump away from Zeus, and clawed Zeus's exposed flank.

Shep stumbled across the windowed floor, pain shuddering up his leg. Zeus fell near the boat's edge, panting. He licked his side, and the slaver that dripped from his jowls was red with lifeblood.

Horrible snapping sounds rose up from the plaza. The lizards feasted like they hadn't eaten in suns. The wild pack wailed in terror. It was a gruesome sight. Shep wondered if even his worst enemies deserved such a fate. *What have I unleashed?*

A howl rose up from a street near sunset. It was Blaze. She bounded into the plaza, tongue lolling, but her stance was fierce. She was ready to tear every wild dog apart. Then more howls, barks, and cries: The whole of the fighting force burst into the space! Hulk, Panzer, Mooch, Paulie — all his strongest fighters tore into the wild pack as if they were toys. And then Shep saw him — little Fuzz, perched on Hulk's shoulders. The cat must have gone after them. *I swear that crazy hairball must have read my mind.*

Shep looked over at Zeus, whose horror showed on his muzzle.

"Smell it, Zeus?" Shep barked. "I'm not just King of the Yappers. I'm King of Every Dog."

Zeus turned his snout slowly, a growl gurgling in his throat. "All hail the mighty king," he snarled.

Zeus jumped at Shep's head, and Shep sank his teeth into Zeus's neck, throwing him down onto the boat. Shep felt like lightning crackled through his muscles now that he had his pack behind him. Zeus rose again, and Shep slammed him down, slashing Zeus's hide with his claws. A third time, Zeus struggled to his paws, hobbling a stretch away from Shep.

"Such a mighty king you are." Zeus's barks dropped from his jaws like slobber between pants. Lifeblood drizzled from his jowls. "Finish me off, Shep. Finish me once and for all."

Zeus stood, one forepaw lifted off the glass, the raw, red meat of it exposed. He closed his eyes and shut his jaws. The last light of the sun shone on his nose. "Good-bye, friend," he moaned.

Shep could down him with a single swipe of his fangs. He was that powerful. And it would be the right thing to do — Zeus had killed so many. No dog would challenge Shep. He was that powerful. He could also let Zeus slink away with his life, and no dog would question him. He was that powerful. He commanded water lizards, he defeated his greatest enemy, he *was* the Champion of the Great Wolf.

"You've done terrible things, Zeus," Shep barked. "But my killing you won't make up for that."

Zeus opened his eyes. His nose dropped, and his sit loosened. A hind leg slid across the slick surface of the boat.

Shep continued, "You have, however, lost the right to live with any other dog. And if I smell you again, I *will* kill you."

Shep turned his back on Zeus. He looked down at his pack of fighters, who were organized and precise. They drove back the water lizards, then finished off what remained of the wild dogs. The fighters tore apart the wild pack, which was nothing more than a horde of untrained and vicious fools. What had he been so afraid of? Those wild mongrels had nothing on his pack of well-trained warriors.

This is why the Great Wolf never killed the Black Dog, Shep realized. *The Black Dog was never a threat to a true pack.*

Shep barked, and his voice echoed around the plaza. His pack gazed up at him with awe. The surviving stragglers from the wild pack scampered off into the shadows, yelping and crying.

"The wild dogs are defeated!" Shep bellowed. His pack howled with him in celebration.

A siren rang out.

Shep couldn't believe his ears. *A siren, a human siren?*

A wild dog came racing down the street back into the plaza. "Humans!" he shrieked as he bolted past.

Some of the pack turned to smell what the wild dog had been running from, tails lifted.

"Master?" Bernie yipped.

It took several heartbeats to register in Shep's mind — humans? But the humans had abandoned their dogs. *They left us to be eaten by the storm.* How could the humans just come back? *And why now, when my pack is finally coming together?* The humans couldn't have planned a worse time to show up.

A point of red light sparkled on the pavement. "The Red Dot!" Waffle barked. "Get the Red Dot!" He ran toward the spark. Just as he reached it, he fell over. Shep thought he saw a metal tooth in Waffle's neck.

The siren blared again — this time, much closer. Flashing red lights pulsed across the buildings. The lifeblood throbbed through Shep's body. These humans were not their masters — these were the men in black who'd raided the fight kennel! These men were not coming to help the dogs — they were coming to hurt them.

"Every dog!" Shep howled. "Into the boat!"

Shep pulled what dogs he could reach up onto the hull with him, while others raced for the crushed floor to get inside.

"Shep!" Zeus whimpered. "Please help me, too." He lurched toward Shep, his hurt paw dragging on the glass.

Shep thrust his shoulder against Zeus's side. "I've got you," he woofed.

Zeus snapped his fangs around Shep's scruff and hauled Shep over, dropping him on his back. Shep hit the floor so hard, the wind was knocked out of him.

"Not good enough for your pack, but always available for your pity, is that it?" Zeus stood over Shep, growling, ready to attack. His bark was a hysterical scream.

Suddenly, Zeus fell limp, his head hitting the windows like a coconut from a tree. A metal dart jutted from his throat. *The humans!*

Shep stayed low, hidden by the raised lip of the boat's shell, and crawled, belly to glass, until he reached the ceiling of the crushed floor. He heard the barks and cries of his packmates caught on the plaza. There was nothing Shep could do, though, against a man in black.

He dropped down and crawled into the main den. The

hand lights of the men flashed through the windows — Shep had mere heartbeats to escape. What dogs had made it into the den cowered in the dark.

"What do we do, Shep?" ChaCha whimpered. Mr. Pickles and several other old timer yappers trembled beside the girldog.

"Follow me," he yipped.

They shuffled through the staircase-hole to the lower floor where the kibble room was. Callie lay in the dark between the shell of the boat and the street below.

"The others have gone," she yipped. "Oscar's leading them out."

"You go, Callie," Shep woofed. "There are more dogs to sneak out."

Callie stood, then dragged herself up into the room. "No, Shep." Her voice was weak. "I have to wait here and hope the humans find me. I need medicine."

Shep waved his nose for ChaCha and the other dogs to squeeze through the window hole. There were so few of them — *How many had been captured?*

"Callie, come with us," Shep woofed. "You don't know these humans. You don't know if they'll help."

"I know that I'm not going to make it without human medicine," she said, coughing.

"We'll figure something out," Shep barked. "Boji might know something."

"Boji's done everything she can," Callie woofed, licking

Shep's nose. "I can't run with the other dogs and you can't carry me the way Honey lugged Fuzz around."

A blur of black fur burst into the room. It was Fuzz, and he leapt onto Shep's neck, screeching. "Hurry, Shep-dog!" he hissed. "Humans in boat!"

"Down the hole, Fuzz," he barked. "I'll follow."

Fuzz nodded his pink nose, then dropped into the dark.

Shep licked Callie's head. "You've made up your mind then, you stubborn yapper?" It was like he was gnawing off a part of himself, to leave Callie behind.

She wagged her tail. "You'd better go."

"I'll come find you," he woofed. "The humans will give you medicine and then I'll rescue you."

Callie grinned, then panted gently. "We'll meet again," she woofed. "I'll be that yapper on the other side of the wall, remember?"

"Shep-dog! Move tail!" Fuzz hissed from deep under the boat.

"I'll come for you," Shep woofed. "Even if it takes a cycle, I'll find you!"

Shep thrust his head into the hole in the floor. The window was made for yappers, not big dogs. Shep shoved one shoulder through. He scratched at the pavement and pushed with his hind legs.

He heard the humans' voices more clearly — they were getting closer to the bottom floor. Callie moaned, hoping to draw them to her.

Shep shifted his chest and drove his other paw and shoulder through the hole. He wriggled his rump and dug with his hind paws. *Almost there!*

He collapsed into the cramped space beneath the boat. The ceiling crushed his back — he had to lie sideways and scuttle through the hole, dragging himself with his forepaws and pushing with his hind legs. He tried to calm his breathing, but it was dark, dark, dark and the space seemed to be getting smaller. *What if I get stuck?*

Lifeblood raced through him. His head began to swim. *No*, he grumbled to himself. *After everything I've been through, I will not die in this cramped cave.*

He pushed on. He heard the humans behind him. He heard Callie give a happy little yap. Then silence. Shep asked the Silver Moon to watch over her. Then he shoved himself forward.

It seemed like he'd traveled a million stretches, but he finally began to smell fresh air, then his paws felt the edges of the cave. Shep pushed himself out into the night.

The cats had dug the tunnel starting from the buildings behind the boat: Shep stood deep inside the rubble that stretched away from the canal. He could barely scent the water.

"Shep?" It was Oscar's tremulous yap. He crept out from the shadows into a sliver of moonlight. When he saw Shep's muzzle, his tail began wagging and his ears pricked up.

"Thank the Great Wolf, you're here!" The pup leapt at Shep's muzzle and licked him again and again.

In between Oscar's kisses, Shep sniffed the air. "How many others made it out?" he asked.

"Me, Boji, Daisy, Rufus, Ginny, Dover, and Snoop." Oscar waved his snout and the seven stepped forward — dark shadows in the darkness.

"And Fuzz," Fuzz meow-barked, hopping down from a ledge.

"There were more," Boji woofed, "but when they heard that the humans were back, they ran to rejoin their masters."

"Those weren't their masters," Shep growled.

"We know," woofed Dover. "That's why we stayed."

"Blaze?" Shep yipped hopefully.

"She-got-captured-by-a-human-Shep-I'm-sorry," whimpered Snoop.

Shep winced, then licked his jowls. "It's not your fault, Snoop," Shep woofed. "Don't be sorry."

Shep jumped onto a broken block of wall. "We have one thing left to do," he barked. "We have to save our friends."

"Like Lassie?" yipped Ginny.

"Just like Lassie," woofed Shep. "It's what an alpha does."

The thrilling conclusion to the
Dogs of the Drowned City trilogy!

THE RETURN

DOGS OF THE DROWNED CITY

DAYNA LORENTZ

SCHOLASTIC

Read on for a preview of *THE RETURN*

About fifteen stretches of open pavement separated Shep from the first cage. In it lay a strange dog, big and brown — and asleep, though it was fully light out. On top of that cage was another, and another small crate rested on top of that. There were two cats in the second cage, a rabbit in the topmost. From this corner, the cages ran toward the cold winds and also toward sunset, farther than Shep could see. The smells of dog and cat and rat and rabbit and bird and Great Wolf knows what else bombarded his nose.

Oscar slumped beside Shep's forelegs, jaw slack beneath his jowls. "It's so big," he moaned. "How can there be so many dogs?"

Shep sat, unsure what else to do. This was too much, this kennel. How could they search all these cages? It would take a lifetime to sniff each one, to find all his packmates . . . to find Blaze . . . to find Callie.

"Fuzz look closer," the cat barked and burst from beneath the last bird-Car. He stopped alongside the corner cage, then sprang onto the top of the first, then the second, and finally onto the roof of the third. The rabbit squealed and scrabbled around its little crate.

Fuzz raced along the tops of the cages and disappeared. Shep dug through his brain for how they could possibly invade this maze of crates, how best to find and free his friends.

"Down!" Oscar cried.

A small bus rumbled toward them along the space of pavement between the winged Car and the cages. Shep ducked deeper into the shadow, hiding himself. The bus drove halfway down the row of cages toward the building, then stopped. A door on its side slid open, and several humans in loose, colorful clothes stumbled out onto the pavement. This bus was followed by others — Cars (open-backed and regular types) and all sorts of machines roared past, dropping off humans and a few dogs and other animals.

"This place is crawling with people," Shep mumbled to himself.

"But not at night," Oscar woofed. He squinted at the cages as if peering into the depths of the maze. "Everything is quieter at night. We could come back then and free all the dogs."

"Oscar, even if we worked from the heartbeat the sun set to when the first tails of dawn wagged, we couldn't open more than a snoutful of cages."

The pup glanced up at Shep, then back at the maze. "A snoutful is better than none."

The sun baked the pavement. Heat rose in steamy waves from the stone. The dog in the corner cage finally woke and lapped up some water. Shep and Oscar stared at his bowl every time he slurped up a snoutful, their mouths dry as sand.

"Could you spare a drop?" Oscar barked to the strange dog. His tiny tongue stuck to the roof of his mouth, distorting his woof.

The dog glanced at him, then at the bowl. "Sorry," he yipped. "The human only comes by once a sun, and I only have enough water for me."

"Can you tell us anything about this place?" Shep woofed. "How many humans are here? How many dogs?"

The dog sniffed the air, then sat. "So many that I never see the same human twice, and more dogs than I've ever smelled. They brought me here in this cage, and I've been in it ever since. Every afternoon, they take me for a walk by the edge of the fence, but other than that, what you see is what I see. Sometimes, strange humans walk by to peer into my cage, but not my girl. Not my family." Suddenly, the dog's ears pricked. He stood and waved his tail. "Have you seen my family out there?"

Shep sighed. "Sorry," he woofed. "I wouldn't know them even if I had seen them."

"But I'm sure they'll be here soon," Oscar added with a cheerful yip.

The dog's tail drooped. He lay down and rested his snout on his paws. "Yeah," he groaned. *"Soon."*

It was nearing midsun when Fuzz dropped down from the piles of cages and raced across the pavement to where Oscar and Shep lay panting in the shade.

"Took you long enough," Shep sighed. "We have to find some water."

"Fuzz find Callie-dog!" the cat meowed. "Callie-dog in building. Have tube in leg."

Shep sprang to his paws. "I'm going in," he woofed.

"Don't be a fuzz head," Oscar barked. "You'd be captured in a heartbeat." He bit Shep's foreleg for extra measure. "We have to find some water, meet back with the others, and come up with some plan that doesn't involve getting caught the heartbeat we set paw in the kennel."

Shep shook his fur, knowing Oscar was right but not liking a woof out of his snout. Callie was here! Callie was in trouble! He had to save her!

"Small-snout right." Fuzz flicked Shep in the nose with his tail. "Shep-dog wait. No help to Callie-dog with fur-for-brain."

They made their way as fast as their paws could manage back to the fence. As they walked, Fuzz explained what he'd seen in the complex.

"Cages in rows, piles of cages. Rodent on cat on dog on dog." His disgust at the arrangement was evident in the tone of his hiss. "But in building, less cages and less dogs. More people. Callie there."

Shep pressed Fuzz for better details of the space, but the cat had little to offer.

"Fuzz no have time to scratch out plan of whole space," he meow-barked. "If Shep-dog want explain better, he go sniff out building himself."

"Then that's what I'll have to do," Shep grumbled.

The others were waiting on the other side of the fence around the toppled tree trunk. It looked like in all those heartbeats, they hadn't moved a paw.

"What did you — *snort* — find?" barked Daisy.

"Yeah-Shep-did-you-find-Callie-and-can-we-go-home-yet-huh?" Snoop leapt against the metal rings of the fence and sent the whole wall shivering.

Rufus nipped Snoop in the hind leg. "Get down before you set the whole mess of humans on us!" he snapped.

Shep smelled that the pack was feeling equal parts anxious and excited. "Did something happen while I was gone?"

"Humans," woofed Dover. "A few drove by in one of those open-backed Cars. They marked the tree." He waved his nose, and Shep saw an orange X painted on the trunk.

Daisy pawed closer to Shep, chest out like she was trying to appear taller. "I ordered the pack to jump into a bush," she grunted. "We stayed hidden."

Daisy was all that was left of Shep's defense team, and apparently she thought this meant that she was in charge when he was away. If the others didn't raise their hackles over the arrangement, Shep wasn't going to make anything of it.

He wasn't sure why the humans painted a mark on the tree, but it couldn't be for anything good. Shep had to get his trapped packmates out of this place and fast.

"We found Callie, so the others can't be far," barked Shep. "Our pack will be back together by sunrise."